LAURIE BOULDEN

Pearl of Persia
Esther's Story
Fruit of Her Hands Series

Laurie Boulden

quotations
from The Authorized (King James)
Version.

Fiction and Literature: Inspirational
Biblical fiction

The cover background is a
photograph taken by the author at Bok
Tower Gardens in Lake Wales, FL.
www.boktowergardens.org

ISBN: 978-1-0881-7169-1

My name is Hadassah. In my Hebrew language, Hadassah means myrtle tree. That may seem odd to you, but for Hebrew tradition, the myrtle tree is a fitting symbol of the recovery and establishment of God's promises. Perhaps by the end of my story, you will see how fitting a name it is.

The story of Hadassah and saving the Jews in Persia has been a favorite of mine since my mother read me a children's story. It was a story I read over and over again. For many years, I've wanted to write my own retelling, and now here it is. I'm so excited to share my vision with you. God empowers an incredibly special woman in a difficult situation. It happened then. It's happened time and again since then. It can happen for you and me today.

A brief language lesson
Foreign terms are used in the story. Want to understand more about what's being said? Use this guide to help you.
Jewish Family Terms

- Mother- Eema
- Grandmother- Savta
- Grandfather- Saba
- Aunt- Doda

Jewish Greetings

- Shalom- peace
- Shalom aleichem- peace be upon you
- Shavua tov- good week

- Chazak u'varuch- be strong and blessed
- Chazak ve'ematz- be strong and courageous
- Yasher Kiach- more power to you

Other Jewish Terms

- Hamantaschen- pastry
- Kreplach- stuffed noodle dumplings
- Shabbat- the Sabbath (last day of the week, Saturday)
- Ketubah- designed marriage contract
- Purim- ritual observance of a day of fasting and a day of festival to celebrate Esther saving the Jews of Persia, takes place in mid-March

Arabic Greeting

- Salaam alaykum- peace be upon you

Other Arabic terms

- Sar Rabu- Great King

Part 1
Chapter: Purim Celebration

Sharine Haftka accepted the hand of her husband, Isaiah, to get out of the car. She could smell the fruit-filled freshly baked cookies from the open corner of the Tupperware box as she held it and the special package beneath her arm. Though a chill wind blew from the northwest, making her glad she'd wrapped the blue scarf around her head and tucked it into the top of her coat, the bare tree she passed boasted tiny buds. The first hint of spring.

Isaiah held her elbow and they climbed the three steps to the porch of their daughter's home. It took one ring of the bell. Sharine smiled as excited shouts rose from within.

"Grandmom's here. Grandpop's here." Feet sounded on the stairs, then across the tiled foyer. She imagined him skidding into the door, which explained the thump and a yell from deep in the house to be careful. Right on que, Sammy opened the door. His dark hair fell over his forehead. His eyes were bright as could be, and he greeted them with a wide smile. Sharine welcomed him into her arms best as she could, then he moved to Isaiah.

"Hi, grandma," Rachel called from the hallway. She took the Tupperware and kissed her cheek.

Sharine patted Rachel's face. "Sweet girl. Surely you remember the Jewish term I taught you last year?"

"Can I have a cookie?" Rachel tried to distract her, but Sharine wouldn't have it.

"My title, dear one. Then you can teach it to your brother." They moved into the hallway and shut the door, cutting off the cold breeze.

"Wasn't it something like Sata or Tata?" She reached for the other package, holding it close as Sharine shrugged out of her coat.

With a grin, Sharine draped the coat across one of Rachel's arms, took her package and box of cookies back. "Savta. Savta Sharine. Repeat it a few times while we take these to the kitchen." She winked. "I'm sure we can let you taste one, to tell me I used the right amount of vanilla."

"Me, too, me, too!" Sammy jumped around them then skipped down the hall to the wide kitchen.

Sharine peeked in the oven. Goodies for their Purim feast warmed on stone cookie sheets. Kreplach meat pies had a better color than last year. She grinned as she set her plate of cookies beside a basket of hamantaschen pastries. With a sniff, she knew her daughter had used the poppy filling.

Rachel leaned across the white and gray marbled counter to peel a corner from Sharine's container of cookies. "Mama let me help make the cranberry and pear chutney."

Sharine offered a triangular cookie to her

grandchildren. "What word are we practicing?" She held the treat just out of reach.

"Savta," Rachel snatched her cookie.

"Hey, wait, what?" Robbie watched Rachel skip away.

Sharine smiled at her beloved. "Savta. Grandmother."

"Savta." Robbie repeated perfectly. "What about grandpa?"

"That would be Saba. When you come this summer, you'll learn a few more words. How does that sound?"

Sammy bit into his cookie shaking his head. "You still have the animals? I wish we had been able to visit last summer. Seems like forever since we were there. Will I get to help feed the chickens?"

"Of course."

"Mother, how are you? How was the drive?" Camille hugged Sharine with a sigh. "Sedgwick decided to get mud on my dress, so I had to change. I'm afraid we aren't quite ready yet."

Sharine grinned. "I know the city has everything a girl could ask for, but I treasure our few hours north into farmland."

"I'm sorry Abe's trip to Disneyland and Doda Talisha's passing kept us from visiting." Camille checked on the warming tray beneath the oven, and then the bread oven. "The braided bread will need another forty minutes."

"No worries, my dear." Sharine patted her hand. "Would you like me to take the children in for the telling of the story?"

"Are you sure? I know Doda Talisha has read for years."

Sharine let the push of sadness take her for a moment, and then squeezed the amulet she'd received at the celebration of life for her sister almost seven months past. She laid her hand upon the wrapped package she'd set beside the cookies.

Camille leaned against her and traced the intertwined circles. "Savta and Saba's Ketubah. Doda Talisha never let me near enough to see it."

Sharine sighed. "Eema spent years converting the original document into her needlepoint. I was afraid Talisha had damaged it somehow and didn't want any of us to know."

Camille smiled. "Maybe someday, you'll be able to get Rachel to appreciate our history. For now, I'll try to get her to sit and listen. Would you like a cup of tea for your reading?"

"Lady Grey?"

"Of course." Camille opened a cabinet. "With a splash of cream?"

Sharine left her daughter putzing in the kitchen and carried her book to the family room. She held one hand against the wall to make the step down. She shook her head at her daughter's vintage eclectic style. The Lawson couch with its curved arm panels in a soft green with flowers remained a bit too stuffy for her. The vibrant, colorful armchair that clashed horribly made her grin. Even with its red tapered legs and multi-toned upholstery, the padded design supported all the body parts that needed more structure. A table had been placed beside it. Sharine pried her shoes off, shoving them under the table, and dug her toes into the shag cream area rug. With its sculptured swirls and scrolls, it pulled the eclectic set of couch and chairs into a comfortable room.

She had just settled into place when grumbling noises moved from the kitchen area into the sunken family room.

"I've heard this story every year since I can remember," Rachel groaned, flopping onto the couch.

Sharine shook her head. "If this is your response at the age of fourteen, you may have heard the story, yet you have never listened."

Sammy rolled across the carpet to his grandmother's feet. "I'm a boy. Do I have to listen to a girl's story?"

Sharine opened her eyes wide. "Is a king not worth your attention? There are murder plots. Battles. Drinking and all the trouble that comes with it." She shook her head. "And if these are not enough, there is the very hand of YHWH. His name is never spoken, yet He is seen in the events at every turn." She sat back. "Come. Let me tell you the story of Esther. It is not what you have heard in Sunday school."

Chapter: Hadassah's Childhood

"Hadassah!" The sound of mother's voice bounced against rocks to echo through the hills.

Hadassah peeked over a rock close to an edge that allowed her to see the field below. Sarae, her mother, stood with one hand on her hip and the other shading her eyes. The scarf wrapped around her head kept her dark curly hair from whipping in the wind like her plum apron. Hadassah waved.

Sarae shook her head. "It is time to go."

Hadassah glanced behind her at the maze of rocks covering the hills where she'd explored for seven years of her life, at least once she could walk. *I do not want to go.* She dared not speak her thoughts to her mother. She squeezed her eyes shut, trying to burn the landscape into her memory. "I am coming," she shouted, then took to the path that would lead her down to the fields. Breathless, she raced to her mother.

Sarae took her hand. "It is only for a season, child. You will return at the harvest moon."

"But I will miss so much. The kits are coming out of the den. Hawks have a nest with eggs in the rocks on the hill."

"Cousin Mordecai will let you bring Tanzia. And he has Opal. You don't know about her, yet."

"Opal?" Hadassah asked as she skipped beside her mother.

Sarae released her hand. "It is a surprise. You will see when we arrive in Susa."

"Is it another cat? Or a dog? Royals have a tiger from India. It could not be anything like that."

Sarae laughed. "I cannot say what it is. All he gave me was a name, lest you should be able to wrest an answer from me and spoil the surprise."

When they arrived at the house surrounded by bare fields, Hadassah watched men load more bags of grains on the second wagon. The wheels creaked from the weight. "Why must we go to Susa? I stayed here with Ishari last year."

Sarae shook her head. "Mordecai visited during the summer. He offered to keep you in the royal city. You will grow to enjoy it." Sarae smiled. "I know how much you like to converse with foreigners. You will meet plenty of them."

Hadassah said nothing more but waited until her father indicated she should climb into the back of the first wagon. She wrapped a blanket around her shoulders as they started to move. The house and surrounding land slowly passed from view as her father led the small caravan toward the King's Highway.

As days on the road progressed, the landscape changed. The rocky hills gave way to plains. Occasional views of water had her standing on tippy toes to see. Sarae set her back down, placing Tanzia on her lap. The young cat rolled and swatted at a ribbon Hadassah pulled from her own braid.

Others joined them as they travelled the highway. Hadassah heard words that made no sense. A boy on another wagon started pointing at things around them, using names Hadassah had never heard. She started whispering those words to herself.

Then came buildings. There was distance between them at first. Toward the horizon rose pyramids, then warehouses with the emblem of a winged bull carved into the stone front. Next came houses and fields, much like the farm she'd grown up on. Then the great royal city, Susa, came into view. Hadassah never imagined such a place. She scooted closer to her mother, leaning against her to whisper, "Why are there soldiers on the wall? Is this a troubled place?"

Abihail, Hadassah's father, laughed. "The king of Persia lives here."

"Is he our king?"

Abihail patted the empty part of the bench beside him. Hadassah scrambled to sit on the elevated seat.

"Many years ago," he explained, "our people were taken from our homeland."

"By this king?"

"No, by King Nebuchadnezzar. I have never seen our homeland. We are the children of Israel. Instead of living in the place of your forefathers, we are scattered across Persia." He glanced at the soldiers as they rolled through the gate into the city. "Perhaps one day our people will be able to return to the land of Abraham, Isaac, and Jacob."

But today wasn't that day. They were entering Susa. Hadassah stared at the new world around her. *Susa is a large city with lots of foreigners*, Hadassah thought as the sound of the wagon wheels changed to a clatter on a hard street surface. For a moment, as noise, color, and scents washed over her, Hadassah longed for the whistle of wind through the rocks and the quiet life as the child of a farmer. The next moment, she noticed thick castle walls jutting from the ground, their rosy hue more the color of a sunset than real stone.

Her eyes were drawn to an archway some stories above the street. Afternoon light splashed perfectly on the man standing beneath the arch. With wide shoulders and dark hair brushing his collar, he stood straight. Red draped from his shoulders. White clung to his legs, disappearing into shimmering black boots. The young man took no notice of the bustling street, but stared ahead, as though caught in a memory.

The sight of him was but a moment. He was royal, though she was unsure as to whom he would be. He looked… forlorn was the word that came to Hadassah's mind.

"Sit down, Hadassah." Sarae grabbed her arm.

"Mordecai's street is back over this way." Abihail slowed their beast as he followed the road to the right.

The city was built house against house. Many, although not all, were two stories. Windows and doors seem to be carved into stone and brick. Abihail made an inquiry, then followed directions a bit further along the street. He drew to a longer house pressed between two others. The second story boasted a balcony.

A man stood in the front garden. She waved as she recognized Cousin Mordecai. To her seven years of age, he seemed old with bits of gray in his beard and wavy hair.

Mordecai smiled, moving to take hold of the pack animals. "Uncle Abihail," he greeted, then grinned at

Hadassah, "and little cousin. Shalom."

Abihail jumped down, then went to the back to assist Sarae. Mordecai took Hadassah's hand. She gauged the distance to the ground and then hopped from her perch.

"You are a brave child." Mordecai approved.

Hadassah tilted her head. "Should I not be brave?"

"Courage is ever a good quality." Mordecai pulled the bag with Tanzia and handed it to Hadassah. "Take her to the garden porch. It is through the main house to the back."

Hadassah skipped. Tanzia's meow expressed displeasure, but the child didn't slow to a walk. The front room of the house was a large open space with several places to sit or lounge. A hanging on the wall drew her attention and halted her trek to the garden. It was a woven tapestry with a landscape of hills and houses in the background. A sun shone out over the land. The beauty of the scene made her wonder where it could be. It looked nothing like the places she knew. Tanzia resumed her meows, which sent Hadassah through a courtyard, then kitchen, then finally to the garden with a covered patio. She sat on a stone tile used to form the ground of the patio. Tanzia took advantage of slack in the bag and jumped out. The young cat shook itself, licked her paw and swiped her ear, and then pounced on a blade of grass that moved in a slight breeze.

"This is a lovely home. You will have a comfortable stay." Sarae said as she joined her daughter. She did not sit but walked into the garden. "Your cousin Mordecai can teach you about plants."

"He also knows about stars and politics." Mordecai interjected as he followed Sarae onto the porch.

"Do you know about little girls?" Hadassah asked as she picked up Tanzia.

"I have three sisters," he nodded. "It is one of them who gave me Opal for a little while. Would you like to meet her?"

Hadassah nodded with exuberance. Mordecai disappeared into the house. Hadassah looked at her mother and they both smiled. Mordecai returned with a small monkey grasping his long vest.

Hadassah's mouth dropped open in wonder as the animal moved. "What is it?"

"A monkey," Mordecai explained. "Yourif, Ati's husband, traded for it. They are going to market and asked me to watch her for a few days."

"I hope Tanzia will like him." Sarae watched the cat, but the black and white feline showed no interest in the monkey, even though it chatted with Mordecai.

Hadassah walked to her cousin and stepped in front of him. She held out one finger and pet Opal down the back. "She is soft like Tanzia." The monkey held onto Mordecai's collar, but looked at Hadassah with large, light brown eyes. Its chatter made it seem to talk to her. She giggled. The monkey reached for the ribbon holding one of her braids. She laughed until Opal yanked her hair.

Mordecai gently drew the monkey's hand away. "She is curious about many things. Let me return her to her room and then we will show you yours."

Sarae wrapped an arm around Hadassah's shoulders. "I think you will enjoy your time in Susa."

Hadassah sighed, resting her head against her mother. "Why can I not come with you? I can help."

"In a few more years." She kissed the top of

Hadassah's head. "Meanwhile, you have our rope of knots to unwind. We will return before you realize."

The room Mordecai provided for Hadassah was on the second floor. A little balcony overlooked the back garden. Though she could hear strange noises from the city, she could not see it, not even the raised palace of Shushan. Walking into her room, the first thing she saw was the basket hanging on the wall near the door. Mother's knotted cord spilled out of it. The bed was on a box with ropes spread across it and blankets and a stuffed mattress to make it comfortable. At the bottom of the bed, a chest would hold her clothes.

"What do you think?" Sarae hugged Hadassah.

"It is different from home, but Tanzia will enjoy the balcony."

Sarae smiled knowingly. "As will you. But no jumping. I don't want to come home and find you have hurt yourself."

Hadassah held her mother's hand, swinging playfully, as they explored more of the house.

***

Hadassah bit her lower lip to keep from crying as Mordecai held her hand. They watched the wagons continue along the street until they turned and disappeared from sight.

He squeezed her hand. "Opal needs to be fed. Shall I meet you in the garden?"

Hadassah nodded. "Does she like mice? Tanzia eats mice."

He smiled. "Opal enjoys fruits."

Not much later, Hadassah bounced as Mordecai brought a basket of figs, apples, nuts, and a hibiscus flower. Opal clung to him, one hand on his collar, the other in his hair, allowing her to peer down at the basket. He set it beside Hadassah. "Hand her one of the figs."

She stood beside him and held the fig to the monkey. Opal jumped on the table, taking hold of the fruit with both hands. She sat and nibbled. The seed dropped to the table, and then she was leaning against the basket for more. Hadassah laughed and handed her the flower. Opal shoved her nose into it, and then ate the whole thing. She seemed content and went to explore the garden.

That evening, Hadassah stared at the timbers of the roof as she lay on the strange bed. It was different, but comfortable. Darkness kept her from seeing the knotted cord in the basket. She rolled toward the balcony. Stars she could see, not so different than home. It didn't take long for her to fall asleep.

***

The sadness causing her to mope the last few days waned. So far, Mordecai had helped her untie four knots. Too many remained. To take her mind from that, she meant to explore the house, to find Opal, but she heard Mordecai talking with someone out front. She listened to their strange words. She still stood at the window when Mordecai returned to the house.

"Good morning. Shalom." He greeted.

Hadassah peered out the window but didn't see the other man. She looked at her cousin. "The words you spoke, why are they different from what we say now?"

He raised one brow. "You listened to us?"

Hadassah nodded. "One of the words you used referred to grains. A boy we met on the road taught it to me."

Mordecai lifted her to sit on a table where they could talk face to face. "It is not proper to listen to conversations that do not concern you. What other words did you learn?"

She told him, pointing when something was nearby.

Mordecai nodded. "These words are of the Aramaic language. It is different than the Hebrew you know."

"Can you teach me?"

"Would you want to learn?"

Her eyes gleamed in a way that made her cousin smile.

Lessons started in the mornings, then Hadassah would practice what she learned as she tended the kitchen garden. On the Sabbath, Mordecai took a wrapped package from an alcove in the stone wall. He unwrapped the colorful fabric, folding it neatly, and placing it on the table. Hadassah leaned up in her chair on her knees, elbows on the table, to look at the object he placed on the fabric. It was about as long as the lower portion of her arm. It had a strap. When Mordecai unhooked the strap, he rolled the object out. From the right side of the page, he began to read. It took her a moment to recognize the story. She'd heard of the two brothers of the first family, but never like this. She stared at the squiggle shapes on the object, and at Mordecai's hand touching the surface and going back and forth. He seemed to be speaking based on what he saw on the object. Respect kept her from interrupting him, but she wanted to learn more.

When he ended the reading and started to roll the object, she placed her hand on top of his. "What is this?"

"The scroll?"

She nodded. "Do those markings have meanings?"

He grinned. "I should not be surprised your interest in language would transfer to reading and writing." He rolled the scroll and used the strap to secure it. "My father taught me to read and write. I found this in a market near the palace. I am not sure how they came to have it. This scroll is precious. The writings of Father Moses are written herein." He wrapped the fabric around the scroll, then returned it to its place in the wall.

"Is reading and writing something I could learn?" She asked, following him into the garden.

He studied her for a moment. "What need would you have to read or write?"

She frowned. "How will I know unless I do?"

At that, Mordecai laughed. "Indeed. I suppose, as we are studying languages, you can learn script. Not sure how much you can learn in the limited time we have."

More days passed. Each morning would start with untying a knot. They would break their fast with bread and honey. Hadassah watched the fruit trees in the garden. Someday soon, they could add an orange for breakfast as well.

Lessons of languages followed breakfast. Mordecai found a slate and a rock that left a mark on the slate and taught her letters. The words they spoke could be captured and written down. Her young mind absorbed all that it could.

After lessons, Mordecai sometimes took her into Susa. Hadassah kept watch as he talked with others. Some were older men to whom Mordecai listened with intent. Some were younger men seeking council with elders. She tried not to listen, instead exploring the marketplace. Covered stalls in a variety of sizes filled the space. Some of the overhangs used plain fabrics while others had chosen differently. Merchants in bright colors let her smell spices from India and Egypt. She stepped around carcasses hanging from hooks.

"We don't often see youth among the stalls." An elder sat holding a cane.

Hadassah found she could understand most of what he spoke in Aramaic.

"I wait on…" She didn't know a word for cousin. "Mordecai."

"He is a learned man. Surely, he is not your tutor?"

"Yes." Hadassah rubbed her hands on her dress. He used a word she wasn't sure of. She tucked it away in her mind to ask about at the next lesson.

"Hadassah?"

She heard her name, smiled, and bowed to the elder, then retraced her steps to Mordecai.

***

"A tutor is someone who teaches, so yes, I am your tutor. Your teacher." Mordecai answered her questions the following morning.

Opal scrambled across the table and scampered onto Hadassah's shoulder. She laughed. "It is a shame your sister returns, and Opal goes home today." She rubbed her fingers on the back of its head. "Do you think you will get your own monkey?"

Mordecai shook his head. "Your Tanzia is easier to care for."

"She enjoys the garden too much. She hardly comes to me for play."

"You go home in a few weeks. She will do better there."

They continued with the lesson. For some reason, the loss of Opal left her downtrodden. Dreams in the night were not all pleasant. Hadassah awoke crying. She pulled the knotted cord from the basket and lay with it bound up in her arms. She slept the rest of the night with it.

***

"Mordecai?" Hadassah frowned then rubbed her eyes. Ropes stretched across the bed creaked as he sat beside her. The sheen of tears in his eyes made Hadassah blink. She remained quiet, waiting.

He swallowed. "There was a raid on the caravan carrying goods to Athens. Took more than a week for news to reach Susa."

"Mother and father were in a caravan. They will not return for twenty-two days." She searched the room until she saw the knotted rope lying across a basket. Every morning… She glanced at the dark window. "It's too early to untie the next knot."

Mordecai pulled her onto his lap. Hadassah rested her head against his shoulder, battling the tightness in her chest.

"They will not be coming home." The sound of his voice shook with heartbreak.

"But they always come home. Last year it was the day before the last knot."

"I am sorry, Hadi. They would return if they could."

Hadassah shook her head, but the tightness spread. Her throat stung and her eyes leaked. She stared at the flame in the lantern Mordecai placed on the windowsill. It didn't help. She cried. Mordecai wept with her.

***

Seven years, and she still kept the knotted rope in a basket beneath the windowsill. Hadassah paid it no attention today. She grabbed a scarf, wrapping her thick brown hair, then racing downstairs. Mordecai sat at the table. She perched on a stool across from him. "Will we

18

see the princes leaving the palace today? What finery their ladies will be wearing."

"There will be no processions. Horrible news reached me this morning."

They turned to the window as a long, low horn blew through Susa. Hadassah grabbed Mordecai's arm. "What has happened?"

Chapter: Vashti's Vanquish

King Ahasuerus, better known by his title Xerxes the Great, glanced across the court of the garden and the collection of people enjoying a feast. Purple cords stretched between pillars held hangings of white, green, and blue. The floor of the courtyard was paved with red, blue, white, and black marble, attesting to the wealth and might of his stature. Success on the battlefront brought pleasure into his thoughts. It was the reason guests had been throughout the palace of Shushan for one-hundred-eighty-seven days. Those closest to the raised platform where he stretched on his lounge were the princes of Persia. Their beds of gold and silver shone in the sunlight.

"My wife is a beauty," Rashid, a prince regent from Lydia, jumped to his feet, a golden cup of wine held high. He stumbled. Men on either side of him grabbed hold, then laughter raised above the singing taking place in a corner.

Xerxes waved his hand. "Beauty? What do you know of beauty?" From his languid position on the dais, he peered across those closest to him. Dark haired princes were arrayed in silver. Dashes of sunlight caused them to glitter as it cascaded through the hanging linens. "My beauty is mine." His jeweled cup felt heavy in his hand, so he drank deeply to lighten it. "Well," he seemed to be talking to himself. "She is mine. But should she also be yours? My queen *is* your queen."

With a fuzzy thought in his head, he rang for Bigtha. The master eunuch arrived. His long pale blue tunic lined with golden threads and gray mantle stood out in its plainness against the brightly hued princes. Xerxes raised his crown and motioned for Bigtha to join them at the royal table. Xerxes blinked, tilted his head, then snatched the jeweled crown from Prince Tarshish of Armenia. The use of white gold allowed blue and green gems to shine. "My queen." Xerxes held the crown to Bigtha. "Our queen. Tell her to wear this and engage us with her beauty."

"This crown?" Bigtha bowed low.

"Yes." Xerxes waved. "It is all the ornament she needs. Let her bare skin be to her compliment."

***

Draperies woven through trees protected the smaller party of women from sight of armed guards. Queen Vashti reclined in a lounge. Her white gown crisscrossed her chest, gathered beneath her breasts, and covered her to her feet. A pair of servants attended each of the women, companions to the princes who entertained with the king. One servant completed the design for a henna tattoo. Vashti's own artist leaned over her hand, working on an intricate scroll across the wrist. Her second servant, Etta, knelt beside the lounge, her face lowered.

"What is it?" Vashti enquired.

"Master Bigtha is here. He comes with a request from the king."

"Does he?" Vashti sat up, careful not to disturb her hand nor the artist adding tear drops. *For the hundred eighty days of celebration and now this last week, he had no need for me? What has changed?* "What would my king request of me?"

Bigtha held the pale crown with its dark jewels toward Vashti. She gasped. "To what do I owe this honor?"

Bigtha bowed his head. "He would like you to wear it."

"But that's--" another woman spoke then silenced herself.

"That is kindness of my lord Xerxes. Please let him know I am honored." She took the crown, surprised both by its weight and its chill.

"He would like you to wear it for him and the other princes. He says you have no need for any other ornament."

From their private time together, Vashti understood what he meant, and her cheeks darkened with red. She glanced at her hand. The tattoo artist had finished the design in the special mineral, but it would take time to set. She directed her gaze on Bigtha. "Inform my lord Xerxes, I am unable to acquiesce to his commandment at this time."

***

The king's face darkened at Bigtha's response. "Take your men and inform our queen we await her presence. All will be forgiven when we hear her steps in the courtyard."

***

Vashti recognized the seven eunuchs at her lounge. She also noticed the other women sitting up, attempting to listen without the appearance of doing so. She kept her voice soft. "Please inform my lord Xerxes I cannot possibly leave my ladies during our ritual. This is not a good time for me."

***

"Am I not her king? Am I not the one who raised her to the position of high queen of Persia? Is it not my right to set her before her people? To have them at awe with her as I have been? Nay, I do not accept her refusal. She is bidden to come. Nay, commanded to appear in her glory wearing the royal crown. I have declared it." He grabbed Bigtha's hand, unmindful of the burn of hot wax, and set his seal upon the palm of the eunuch. "Show her this. Where your words fail, my strength shall prevail."

***

Vashti snapped for her servant to attend to the wound on Bigtha's hand. She looked at the other eunuchs whose grave faces did not move her. "Inform my esteemed king I cannot possibly attend his request."

"My lady," one of the smaller men stepped closer. "He is not reasoning well. It is not wise to offend him further."

"Offend?" She scoffed. "He is drunk. Let him sleep and dream. I will approach him when he has returned to reason."

"But my lady…"

She refused to let him say more. "Be gone. My answer is final. We will meet when he is better."

***

Xerxes' roar silenced the room. All seven of the chamberlains scuttled from his sight. "What should I do? Is this to be born?"

"It is worse than you think." Prince Memucan of Cissia stood. "Each of us brought a woman who now sits with Vashti. They have witnessed her refusal. What is to stop them from refusing to obey in their own homes? Or teaching within each province how women need not follow the bidding of their husbands and fathers? What chaos she has wrought. Are each of our homes to become a battle ground because the king allowed our queen to refuse his commandment?"

"What do you suggest?" With passion that could only come through consumption of spirit upon spirits, the princes and Xerxes devised a great punishment.

The royal commandment signed by each of the princes ripped Vashti from her position and possession of her royal estate.

"This is foolishness," Vashti didn't care that streaks of kohl and mascara ran down her cheeks as her tears poured. She struck at the soldiers removing her from her home forcibly.

The soldier, Sether Mehl, did not find Vashti particularly attractive. Nor did he care a drunken stupor fed the actions of the king. Another better than she would take her place as queen. He'd heard those words. His sister was better than Vashti. In one fell swoop, he drew his sword and thrust into the queen. Vashti's eyes widened. As she fell to the ground, blood pooled around her hands, darker than the henna paste that had yet to be wiped from her hand and wrist. She gasped for air once, and then she lay still, staring blindly at the sky.

***

"Wait," Sammy sat up. "They killed her? Because she wouldn't do what the king said?"

Sharine pressed her hand against the Word. "Evil

kills in many ways. None of them are good. The power of the spirit of alcohol can turn the mind of a wise man." She shook her head. "No one ever called Xerxes wise."

Rachel stopped Sammy from further comment. "Let her go back. What does Hadassah have to do with this?"

***

Xerxes groaned at the pain in his head, but at least his head no longer swam. The jeweled cup beside him held water. No more wine. He waved for Bigtha's assistance. Bigtha winced as Xerxes gripped his hand to stand. Xerxes frowned. "What happened?" He turned Bigtha's hand over and saw the red welts and blisters in a circular shape. "Who did this?"

Bigtha glanced down at the red tile on which he stood.

"I demand your answer. Who?"

"My lord, you did."

"Me?" Xerxes gulped. "Why would I?" He searched the courtyard. Persian princes slept on beds covered with light blankets. Commoners lay on the ground. No one stirred. It had been a long, drunken week. He narrowed his gaze on Bigtha. "Why would I do this?"

Bigtha sighed. "You were displeased with Queen Vashti's repeated refusal to come naked for you and the princes' pleasure."

Xerxes wanted to rub his head, but to do so would undermine his providence. "Is she in the women's quarters? Tell her I will meet with her alone."

Bigtha tugged on his gray mantle. "She is dead."

"What?" Xerxes' heart thudded painfully. "How? By whose hand?"

Bigtha indicated a scroll half hidden by a tapestry that had been pulled down.

"Send me a priest, the one who wrote this." He stared at the scroll, loath to pick it up. Shadows of memories shifted in his mind. The princes began to stir. He glanced at Rashid. "Stay."

The prince looked uncomfortable as he sat on the bed.

"My king," a priest bowed beside him.

"You wrote that?" He pointed at the scroll.

The priest picked it up. "Yes, my lord."

"Who told you what to write?"

"The princes worded most of it. Your wroth was great."

Xerxes closed his eyes. "What did they say?"

"They removed Vashti as high queen. Couriers have been sent to each province for each prince, commanding women to obey their husbands and fathers on point of death."

"Vashti is dead. How did that happen?"

"She did not want to leave."

Fury burned through any pain he felt. "Guards!" His bellow stirred the courtyard. Captain Hithem hurried to his side.

Xerxes pointed at the scroll. "Any whose sign appears on this is to be taken to the hill and staked." He noticed a look between the priest and soldier. "Save my own."

Prince Memucan ran to him. "Xerxes, you cannot mean--"

Xerxes slammed his hand across Memucan's face. "Out of my sight. All of them, out." He glared at Captain Hithem. "The one who killed her, take him and be especially mindful of the stake." He turned back to the others. "Your plot has taken my queen. You thought there would be no repercussions?" Fury made him shake.

Captain Hithem grabbed the young man. The priest pointed at the other princes. Most were grabbed from sleep.

Afternoon waned when Xerxes went to the balcony where the hill could be seen. Seven princes and a soldier hung impaled. On one, the stake pierced through the neck and his head hung at a strange angle. With the others, stakes penetrated through to their mouths, and there they would stay until their bodies no longer twitched.

***

Mordecai stopped Hadassah from leaving the house. "Remain here until the bodies have been removed."

Hadassah shook. "Why would he require such acts?"

Mordecai frowned. "He is king of Persia. The life of us all is in his hands."

She sat across from him. "Will he choose a new queen?"

"The queen mother has her residence in the palace. There is no immediate need for another queen."

"Will provinces revolt for the death of their princes?"

"You think further than our king," he smiled. "There will be weakness, whether real or perceived. I fear outside forces will seek to draw us into another war."

"Is that what they say in the palace?"

"My position there is not so great. Master Altier is a minor advisor."

"He has you to make him great." Hadassah kissed the top of his head, and then went through to the garden to look for the cats.

Chapter: A Plan to Encourage the King

There was battle with Greece, and a great defeat that tore at King Xerxes, embittering his soul so that life in the palace grew dark and strained.

"He will have us all killed if we do not devise a plan," Zethar hissed to Carcas.

"What would appease him?" Carcas smoked his pipe.

"Something to take his mind from his troubles. A new queen, perhaps?" Zethar grabbed Carcas' arm. "Or a competition to gain a new queen. Something that would require his attention for a long time."

Carcas nodded. "We know how he likes women. Provinces are still unrestful though it has been three years since the death of their princes. Bring women from all the provinces, no matter how far. Even if he does not choose one for his queen, they will become part of his harem."

Zethar stilled. "Great honor will be bestowed on the family and province of the new queen. We must find Bigtha. He will know if this is a worthy plan."

***

"Blessings of the gods bring you peace."

Xerxes turned from the long window overlooking Susa at the sound of his mother's voice. "What are you doing here? I thought you were in Hadis."

"I arrived a few days ago and have been refreshing myself from my travels."

"You heard of our defeat at the straits of Salamis. Our navy has been decimated." He flung himself into a chair. "Vashti has cursed us."

Atossa scoffed. "Your father suffered defeat in Greece as well. It is the whim of gods, not of curses that determine such courses."

"I do not know what to do."

"There is an empire surrounding you. Giving position to those provinces whose princes you killed has stemmed risks of retribution. Your chamberlains have an idea that may lift your heart."

He looked at her. Atossa appreciated gold. Her skin had been dusted with it and threads of gold contrasted with her royal burgundy gown. "They have spoken to you of a plan?"

"They thought it… expedient to ask my opinion before approaching you."

"You should tell me."

"It is not my place," she lowered her head, "but know I approve."

Xerxes drummed his fingers on his chair. "Are they near?"

Atossa grinned. "They will not be difficult to find. Shall I send them to attend you?"

He glanced out the window where an orange hue colored the sky as the sun lowered beyond the hills. Anything that could take his mind from the throws of failure and death would be good. "Yes, they may attend. Join me for a late evening meal and we can discuss their idea."

Orange had faded to the faintest gleam when Bigtha and Carcas entered. Insects serenaded the twilight. The eunuchs bowed, and then Xerxes waved for them to sit on cushions close to his chair. "Queen mother requested an audience for you to speak. I granted her request."

The younger servant looked to Bigtha, who swallowed before standing to speak. "Most blessed king, your countenance has fallen of late, and our hearts darken because of it. By our reverence and adoration, we would have you lift your spirits. We have thought long and hard on what we might do."

"Really?" Xerxes' foot moved restlessly, and his lips thinned.

Bigtha hurried on. "Oh, my lord, your countenance is lowered for you have no queen to lift it up. Our thought is to let beautiful young virgins be sought. You can appoint officers in all the provinces of Persia to gather their beautiful young virgins to the harem in Shushan. Put them in the custody of Hegai, your eunuch in charge of the women. Let their cosmetics be given to them. The young woman who pleases the king shall be queen. The others remain in your harem to raise seed to the house of rulers of Persia."

Xerxes remained quiet. Bigtha returned to his cushion. There were women in the harem already, but no one who captured his attention as *she* had. He did not want to think of her name. Could another woman drive her out of his heart and mind? What joy would be felt by the province whose young woman became the new queen. Great reward would be given to them. He stroked his beard as he contemplated the task. "Each province provides their most beautiful young women?"

"Yes, my lord, over a period of time. We stagger their arrival to the palace."

The competition would be something different. No fear of defeat. Spice up the harem. Someone would be queen, but he would have plenty of beautiful companions. He relaxed his lips. "Your idea intrigues me. Who would help develop this plan? We need someone who can organize and get things done. Someone who will understand the needs."

Bigtha nodded. "We require a team. Master Hegai has knowledge of the women quarters."

Carcas lifted his hand. "Queen mother," he bowed in Xerxes' direction. "If you agree."

"Master Ristel, one of your advisors." Bigtha added.

Xerxes shook his head. "Not Ristel, he is too old. Choose a younger advisor, Meise, perhaps."

"What of a scribe? We can prepare an announcement to go to each of the provinces along with the officers."

At this, Xerxes agreed. "A scribe is appropriate, but I want a review of the plan before anything is sent."

Both men stood and bowed. Bigtha said, "Our pleasure is to serve you, oh king. May the gods favor you this day and always."

Xerxes waved them off. "Do as you have bid. Return with your plan."

***

The group met on the terrace of Queen Mother's residence. Her guards stood as silent sentinels just beyond the pavement. A raised deck with a jewel-toned chair provided the elevated status for Atossa. Master

Hegai held the next highest place of honor. Soveign and Cornelius, advisors to Xerxes, had seats at the table further from the queen. Hegai had invited three tradesmen: a builder, a merchant, and a scribe to record their proceedings. These three sat at the end of the table.

Atossa peered at Hegai. "Pray explain why such are seated near me."

Hegai stood, bowing his head as he spoke. "Mother of gods, I do not disrespect the high honor due you. The needs of such a project in the expedited time we have require skill and knowledge that is beyond us."

Cornelius nodded, and Atossa motioned for him to stand.

He, too, kept his face lowered. "There may be hundreds of women who come. Each province will be eager to claim the new queen. Each candidate will require a time of preparation. We want the king to be pleased. Our purpose must be to enhance the natural beauty of the women when they are here."

Atossa motioned for him to sit. "Preparations for the harem take a year. Do you propose each woman receives the same preparations? The materials needed will be staggering."

"Which is why we have a merchant at the table. He will address our need for oils, cosmetics, and food. The builder will evaluate the structures currently in the women's quarters and determine what we need to build to accommodate our candidates and their maidens."

Soveign lifted his hand. "Someone needs to coordinate among everyone. Master Altier, one of the lesser advisors, has an assistant named Mordecai. He would do well with such a task. I have used him myself on occasion."

Atossa stood and the others jumped to their feet. "Have your plans. You will do more without me here. I will meet with Hegai later today to go over what has been decided." She peered at each person around the table. "Before you take your plan to my son."

"As you wish," Hegai's deep voice spoke for them all.

***

Twilight darkened the sky before Hegai requested an audience with Atossa. Torches flickered throughout her room. She sat on a carved wooden chair with cushions. A cat purred in her lap as she groomed it with a short comb.

Hegai bowed. "Forgive my arrival at the late hour. Our plans were long in coming."

She motioned for him to sit across from her on another chair exactly like hers. He hesitated a moment at the unfamiliar honor then did as directed. "The women coming in need to be separated from the harem. The western most wing will work. Not even the gardens are shared. But the size of that wing is in no way adequate. We can build an additional hundred and twenty suites, both in the western wing and on the harem. The king will not want to release the women he has taken."

"There may be children as well, so increase the gardens around the harem." Atossa nodded.

Hegai bowed. "We need storehouses for oils. Workhouses will hold seamstresses. Additional kitchens will be added. We need a year to prepare. Merchants gather supplies. During that time, our officers make plans for each province. Selections will be recorded. Each candidate will have an appointed time. We stagger them. When they arrive, they have a year of preparations.

I will oversee the targeted needs of each of them. Each group has a master guide, one of the class of eunuchs, to arrange necessary maidens to care for the virgins."

Atossa let the cat jump from her lap and then shook her long skirt. "You have thought of everything. Thank you for indulging my need to know." She paused for a moment, her foot tapping on the tile floor. "How will they meet with the king?"

"Each has her night, sometime after their year of preparations."

Atossa sighed. "Most of them will spend their lives in the harem. What will they have to compensate for their sacrifice?"

He tilted his head. "What do you suggest?"

"There are galleries of jewels and treasures. Every gown I have ever worn is stored away. Let them choose what they will and take it with them to the king."

"Even to keep afterwards?"

"Indeed." Atossa smiled. "It is a small payment for their lives and may serve them as they adjust to harem life."

"You provide a generous gift."

She lifted a brow. "Nothing will be taken from the citadel." She smiled. "Your plan is well-met. Take it to the king in the morning. He will direct you."

LAURIE BOULDEN

36

Chapter: Preparing for competition

Mordecai's heart sank when he saw Hadassah run down the stairs. At fifteen, his cousin-daughter's beauty had few rivals. In a year, she would be old enough to be selected by officers of Susa.

"Well, what news?" Hadassah hurried to place a cup of tea by Mordecai's chair. Though she shook from excitement, she stood respectfully until Mordecai pulled off his outer cloak and sat. She plopped on the floor by his feet.

"I have heard nothing. Have the birds made a report for you?" He teased.

She rolled her eyes. "You have learned something." She stilled to study him for a moment. "A great many things by the weight of concern in your eyes."

He sighed. "There will be a search for a new queen."

"That is a good thing." Hadassah grinned. "Why are you concerned?"

"Young women will not have a choice to participate in the competition."

"To be chosen queen would mean high honor."

Mordecai took a drink, but the hot liquid did not calm his mind. "Only one queen, chosen from possibly hundreds of young women. Plans are not to release the women when they do not please the king. They will live in the harem."

Hadassah considered the implications. "All but the queen become slaves to the king's fancy?"

"The queen does not hold as much power as she may think. As Queen Vashti discovered."

"But still, she will have more freedom than any of the others. I am grateful I am no beauty."

"Hadassah," Mordecai shook his head. "You grow more beautiful each day. The selection process does not begin for a year. You will be chosen."

Hadassah scoffed, but Mordecai held no doubts.

***

"He manages with skill. Why has he not been raised to the level of advisor?"

"He is a Jew."

Mordecai had been working in Shushan for months. Hearing the reason he had not gained a higher position caused something within him to straighten. He heard a laugh.

"They are a conquered people who should have remained slaves. Nonsense making them anything more."

Mordecai moved from behind a great pillar.

"Ah, Mordecai," Carcas walked in his direction. "May the grace of the gods shine on you this day."

Mordecai smiled. "I feel I do not seek anything from the gods of Persia. Many of my people hold to our own beliefs, even in exile."

"I had not realized." Carcas did not seem overly concerned. "I wanted to meet with you because this man has offered his service, to assist with the countless details to which you must attend." The young man stepped forward and Carcas introduced him. "This is Haman, of the Agagite house."

Mordecai blinked, but kept his face pleasant as he peered at Haman. "Your offer is appreciated, but I have no need for your aid."

Haman frowned. "Are you refusing me?"

Mordecai did not bow to the hard gaze of Haman. "We are weeks from accomplishing the goals we have set. It would be foolish to bring in another at this point."

"Well," Carcas placed his hand on Haman's shoulder. "His point is valid. A sign of the quality of his thinking." He nodded to Mordecai then returned his attention to Haman. "There will be other opportunities as the competition gets underway."

Haman smiled for Carcas, but his eyes burned with emotion when he looked at Mordecai. "I thought I would help. Forgive my intrusion." He walked away before Mordecai could respond.

Carcas laughed. "He aspires to high places. If he gains the king's attention, he will get there. He is just the sort Xerxes appreciates."

"Thank you for the introduction. I spoke with oil merchants. Their product can last two years, much longer and a bitter turning may happen. The warehouse will be full at the spring festival when the first wave of candidates arrives."

Bigtha joined them as they walked the outer corridor of Apadana, the immense audience hall of Shushan. "Officers leave tomorrow. The first round of virgins will arrive in a month."

Mordecai frowned. "The month of Tevet? Is it safe to travel in winter? Would it not be better to wait until spring?"

Carcas glanced behind him, then lowered his voice to respond. "Hasiyatis, month of the worship of fire. It is best to use the Persian calendar. Today is Ahura Mazda, worship of the great creator."

Mordecai placed his hand on his chest. "I speak for myself. Many calendars are used throughout the provinces, based on who they once were. It is an element of planning that has been most challenging."

"Our winters are mild, compared with those provinces to the north. They should be pleased to travel here."

Mordecai smiled. "I am pleased we do not get the white rain. Have the officers received the gold leaflets with the king's seal? The gold will be little compensation for their daughters, but it is something to remind them of the honor of the competition."

"Yes, the scribes completed those yesterday." Bigtha handed Mordecai a small wood box with a design of lines and scrolls. The wood gleamed with oil. "Your service is greatly appreciated. Please receive this as a token."

"I am honored." Mordecai rubbed his hand across the Khatam pattern.

He gave the box to Hadassah the day they received the golden seal indicating her selection to the king's harem. No tears clouded her eyes, although Mordecai had to control his. Her attention focused on the small paper with its raised wax emblem. He sat and motioned for Hadassah to settle nearby.

"We knew this moment would come. I must speak with you about an important matter." He held his hand out for the seal. She slowly gave it to him. He placed it on the table beside his chair. "I have given great thought and prayer to this matter. You must be afforded every opportunity to gain the king's favor and be selected as the new queen of Persia. I fear if the people in charge knew you are Jewish, some will do all in their power to see that you fail. You must not reveal your people or kindred."

"Not? But you are my family, like a father. How can I not make it known?"

Mordecai took her hands. "It is a hard secret I ask of you, but you must obey me in this. I have been your teacher. If any is to know there is something between us, it is to be that."

"My name will give me away. Hadassah is not of Persian origin."

"I have thought on that as well. You have been the star of my world since your parents died. I am sorry for their passing but raising you has been great joy for me. I am proud of the young woman you are becoming. The Persian name I feel will most complement who you are, is Esther."

"Esther?" She repeated the name softly, her chest aching.

"Yes, that is who you must become. Esther."

***

The days passed too quickly. Mordecai's part of preparing for the women ended, and he returned to assisting Master Altier. But even in the courts beyond Shushan, where lesser advisors worked unless directed to the upper courts, they could feel the tinge of preparations. Fifteen young women of Susa were selected by the king's command. Excitement buzzed through the marketplaces. Visitors from far provinces, most likely to have never visited the capital of the Persian Empire, would have needs and wants. The reward for the family and province of the new queen became legendary.

Hadassah frowned at her friend Meisha. "An entire family is not going to be given a palace nor gain a royal guard, and our streets will not be finished in gold. Can you imagine how slippery that could be in the rain?"

"I am to marry David. We are betrothed. How can I go?" Tears wet her cheeks.

"We've heard the edict read by the priests. It clearly indicates young *virgins*." Hadassah wanted to roll her eyes as Meisha's cheeks flamed. "Move up the wedding. It is the only way."

Not having her friend with her in Shushan would make keeping her family a secret easier. Esther. She repeated the name to herself. It was different, but not unpleasant.

Chapter: My Name is Esther

The day to go to the palace came. Mordecai held her close for a moment. "I cannot go with you. My tears will give too much away."

Hadassah wiped her damp cheeks. "Chazak u'varuch."

He kissed her forehead. "Chazak ve'ematz."

She took a deep breath. She would need strength and courage in great supply.

Mordecai walked with her as far as the upper streets. From there, she went on alone. She turned the corner of the stone wall. In front of her, a great arch of iron marked the opening into the woman's compound. The gate of scrolls and birds spread wide in invitation, but most of the young women inside did not look as though they wanted to be there. Some cried. A few tugged uselessly at the guard assigned to hold them.

In her heart, Hadassah understood their fear, but the king's edict could not be ignored and there was a crown to be won. She entered the fray on a wave of calm. Hadassah compared herself with the others. Her simple gown swished against her sandaled feet. Many others were elaborately dressed. Colors were wonderful, although one girl's shade of green made her look sick. Hadassah had done nothing to her hair, letting it tumble down her back. The sides were pulled up with a bone clip. Many of the others were the same. Managing a delicate hair design while traveling was no easy feat. The woman with the awful green dress wore a turban that seemed to swallow her head.

Hadassah carried a bag with her, holding the charm her mother had given her inside the box from Mordecai, and something else she hoped to get inside. She moved forward with small steps, observing. What first appeared as mayhem was indeed orchestrated. There were groups of young women spread across the courtyard. Priests lingered beside scribes holding scrolls for recording details. A different group of women waited closer to the buildings. Not all were young, though the colors of skin were as broad as the rest of the courtyard. The few men in the area were soldiers, priests, or servants. A tall man with ebony skin stood near a fountain. His gray mantle marked him as a member of the Order of Eunuch. He pointed at a soldier, directing him to move his charge toward the line into the southern wing of the women's quarters. Hadassah moved toward him.

"May the sun bask upon your health and well-being," she greeted in traditional Persian.

"And may the moon shine its radiance upon you with many blessings." The hard lines of his face eased slightly.

"My guardian had business in the council room and dropped me near the gate." Hadassah looked around. There had to be at least fifty young women mulling about. "I am not sure what I should be doing."

"How far have you traveled?"

"Not far at all. We live in Susa."

He nodded at the various visitors. "Some of them have come hundreds of leagues."

Hadassah noticed a young woman on a nearby bench clutching a cylinder-shaped pillow of red silk. Dark smudges beneath her eyes showed she'd started the day with kohl, but tears and subsequent wiping had smeared the dark colors. "She must be tired and fearful. May I talk with her?"

The eunuch smiled. "Please do, although her language may be different than our own."

Hadassah moved to the girl. Though her weeping was subdued, the misery of her gaze caused Hadassah to feel pity. She knelt beside her. "Good morning."

The girl shook her head, fresh tears pooling in her brown eyes. "I do not understand any of you."

Hadassah placed a hand on her leg. "My cousin taught me many languages. Are you from the Indian borders?" She easily recognized the Indian language.

Hearing someone who could understand her brightened the girl's countenance. "None of my attendants were permitted to enter with me. They keep asking me questions. I don't know how to answer them."

"How would your companions be recognized?"

She gulped. Her eyes were shaped like almonds, tapering upward on the outside. Crying had puffed them, but she seemed calmer. "We traveled in a red wagon with the emblem of the great dragon embellished with gold."

Hadassah smiled. "Should be easy to locate. Let me speak with our host."

She found the same man talking with a pair of servants. Standing beneath the shade of an olive tree, she watched. The serving men were younger, but they watched the dark man, nodding at his direction. Their respectful demeanor did not diminish once they turned from him. The dark man elicited respect. Hadassah stored the information in her mind as she stepped forward. "May the blessing of gods be with you." She bowed her head.

He smiled. "Did you find you could talk with our little friend?"

"I did. She speaks an Indian language, Prakrit."

"Are you from India?"

"No. I am of Persia. My teacher thought I had a knack for languages. I learned well."

"Do you understand Egyptian?"

She nodded. "That I learned from a servant in our house. Before my parents died."

"Do you have maidens to assist you?"

"No. I am here alone."

He considered Hadassah for a moment, then nodded. "An Egyptian oils mistress arrived yesterday. She struggles to understand Aramaic. I will assign her to you."

"Thank you," Hadassah glanced across the courtyard. "Why will I need an oils mistress?"

"You will learn much once you have settled. What is your name?"

"Esther." It was her first use of the name Mordecai had selected. With a breath, she released the name of Hadassah and took Esther as her true self.

"Ah," he nodded. "Star. One who shines. I feel you may be the brightest star among us. I am Hegai, master of the women. If you have any need, please let me know."

Esther smiled. "If you have a need for my

understanding of languages, please let me know."

"There is one." Hegai led Esther to a grove of trees in the southern corner of the women's courtyard. Four soldiers stood at attention. Among the trees sat a young woman. Her back was against a trunk, and she stared toward the outer wall. With her arms crossing her chest, stiff posture, and thinned lips, the girl didn't need to speak her displeasure.

"Who is she?"

He shrugged. "They forced her from the carriage, then it left."

"I can try." Esther stepped out of the shining sun into the shadows of the trees. With the breeze from the east, the area was slightly cooler. She settled against a tree a few feet away. "Are you well?" She tried the greeting in Aramaic first, then Egyptian. Prakrit elicited no response. She tried Jewish. There was a flicker. Esther smiled. "You are of Jewish descent?"

"What does it matter to you?"

"We are all of us here at the king's bidding."

"I am a servant. His bidding does not apply to me."

"They've been confused by so many arrivals. I don't think they expected the different languages."

Her arms remained crossed, but she faced Esther. "How did you learn the Jewish language?"

"I had a good teacher. What is your area of service?"

"I grew up working in kitchens. Mother says I'm an artist." Her lips thinned even more. "I'm certain that is why I have been brought here."

"I could use a food artist. Would you consider working for me?"

"Better than trapped in the trees with four soldiers guarding my every move."

"Let me speak with Hegai. See what we can do."

The woman took a moment to breath, then nodded. "My name is Esme."

"I am Esther."

Esme tilted her head. "I thought you would have had a Jewish name."

Esther smiled. "This is who I am now." She motioned for the nearest soldier to pull her to her feet. His cheeks and ears reddened, but he assisted. Esther went in search of Hegai.

***

Esther held her bag tight as the line of women moved into the southwest wing. Built in a hurry, the long hallway, although wide, had no decoration. Its color was that of dry bricks. Arched doorways lined both sides of the corridor. On the left side, Esther noticed a girl standing in a shaft of light inside her room.

"It's small."

"They'd have to be. I heard they have nearly a hundred girls already. And more are coming."

Esther overheard streams of conversations. From what she could tell, the rooms weren't small. They had windows. Several mats leaned against a wall in an alcove formed by the arched opening. The rooms had to be large enough for servants to sleep as well.

Continuing, the number of women in the group dwindled. When they reached the end of the wing, a silent slave opened a door. Stepping through, Esther could tell they moved into the older part of the women's compound. The entire hallway was arched with colorful tiles covering the ceiling, giving the appearance of moving water. Instead of individual rooms, the area had suites. In the first few sections they passed, each arched opening had two doors.

Esther was the only one remaining when they reached another door held by a silent servant. She hesitated. "I'm sorry, did I miss my room?"

The older eunuch, not Hegai, waved for her to follow. There were stairs, but he paused at a simple wood door. "This leads into the gardens. Yours is the only suite with an access door. All the others have to go around the courtyard to get to the gate leading into the garden." He took a key from his pocket and unlocked the door, allowing it to swing open. Two tall green hedges flanked a pathway made of large, round, flat stones. He closed the door, locked it, and held the key to her. "You may explore later."

He led her up a flight of stairs, and Esther squeezed her hand tight around the top of her bag. The area was opulent. Tiled scenes filled the ceiling. Murals of dancers lined the walls. There were benches and padded stools. Straight ahead was a double set of doors in an oversized arch. He moved ahead, flung them open, then beckoned her to follow. "This is where you will sleep." He barely gave her time to ogle the bed before leading her to an alcove with an indoor toilet. The room went past the outer wall to allow waste to drain.

"Is there a tub for washing?"

"That is in the next set of rooms." He led her back through the double doors to the hallway. On the right, he opened the first door. There were a series of three closets and then a water room. "Then down here," he wasn't giving her any time to linger. "Down here are all the rooms for your seven maidens."

"Seven? I only have two."

"There is time to select your other five."

The size and luxury of the section filled her with wonder. "Why have I been given this space?" Esther stopped in the middle of the corridor.

He turned with a smile. "Someone has to live here. Why not you?" A soft meow from her bag drew his attention. "No one said anything about live animals."

Esther held the kitten against her chest. "She was too young to leave alone."

The servant frowned. "Still do not know what to do with her."

"I am used to taking care of her."

"Will she want to go outside? The little thing will get lost." His eyebrows lowered. "And there are hawks."

"I will keep her indoors."

"No." He thought a moment. "The gardeners can build another greenhouse close to your private entrance. They can do a variety of grasses. She will be safe."

Esther rubbed the kitten beneath its chin. "You are generous beyond thanking."

The older man shook his head and turned away while muttering to himself. "At least it is not one of those wild cats."

Chapter: Esther Begins Preparations

Sounds were different. Esther lay on the wide bed, unfamiliar cushions keeping her from the hard floor, with a woven cover to keep out the cold. She lay with one arm bent beneath her head, staring at diamond shapes in the ceiling. Sconces by the toilet room remained lit, allowing light to flicker through the room. The kitten curled against her side and did not move when Esther shifted. How were others faring? Did they have blankets for their mats to keep the cold from the floor away? Did they have a tray of food with a wide selection of fruits and cheeses? A pitcher of wine? At least Esme and Khepri had beds. Not as opulent as her own, but they should have covers to keep them warm through the night.

She must have fallen asleep, because next she noticed real light dancing on the walls. The windows were open. A girl with a wide face and long wavy hair tied curtains to the wall. "I hope your sleep was blessed with much rest. You have a busy day ahead."

Esther sat up. "What am I needed for?"

The girl smiled brighter. "I am Jasmine. I've been

assigned as your companion."

"Glad to meet you. Were you among the other arrivals yesterday?"

"Oh, no, miss. I have been blessed to serve the Queen Mother Atossa. Master Hegai requested of her."

Esther grinned. "You are familiar with the palace?"

She nodded. "And grounds. We will get you where you need to be."

"I am honored."

"The honor is mine, Miss."

"Please, call me Esther."

"That would not be right."

"As my companion, I must insist." A meow sounded, and she swept up the kitten into her arms.

Jasmine's eyes widened. "What have you there?"

"She was too young to leave. I had to bring her. Master Eldij has offered to build a cage for her in the garden. Large enough for the two of us to play. Her name is Cleo."

"Does Esme know to bring food for her?"

"Have you met Esme? Is she in better spirits?"

Jasmine nodded. "The other woman as well, though I didn't know how to ask her name."

"Khepri. She is beautiful. Her skin is much smoother than mine."

"That will change."

Esther tilted her head. "How?"

But she revealed no more. "Ah, Parisa has come. She will help you dress."

"I don't need help dressing."

"Mistress," the new woman floated closer. "We all need help; we just don't realize." She took a breath. "You will find every aspect of your life must change. You are in the palace with hope to win the crown. Follow me."

Esther did as she was told. She dropped Cleo on the bed but noticed Jasmine pick her up as she turned. Parisa was taller and walked with a gate that seemed to glide. She wore a blue suit with a matching scarf. She led Esther to the wardrobe rooms. Already, outfits she didn't recognize hung on the walls.

"Modesty is an appropriate manner in the world, especially as a royal concubine. More so as queen." Once again, she breathed. "There will be no modesty here. Our purpose is to prepare you from the heart outward to be queen. Turn around."

Esther obeyed, somewhat taken aback as Parisa undid the ties of her nightgown.

"Your figure is divine." Parisa assessed by walking in a circle as Esther stood naked. "Hegai will evaluate the condition of your skin and what is to be done." Parisa selected a yellow gown. "This warm tone will complement your dark hair. When was your last menstrual cycle?"

Esther battled with the urge to cover herself as she answered. "Two weeks."

Parisa nodded. "We will work with your cycle. There are herbs to modify, as needed. Here, put the drawers on. Use the strings to tie them to stay in place."

The thin fabric had wide legs and came up to her waist. Without ties, they would have fallen off.

"Raise your arms." Parisa pulled the yellow gown over her head. "Have a seat while I tie this undergarment. You'll need a little more room in the chest."

Esther sat. of course, she'd known there would be rituals and preparations, it had just never occurred to her what those would entail. "Where in Persia are you from?" She made conversation.

"How does that feel?" Parisa asked as she tugged on an under tie.

Esther straightened. The top part of the gown fit well. "I like it."

"I am from Calliha."

"On the Mediterranean? I have wanted to visit."

Parisa hooked one side of a scarf at the shoulder then swept it down and around to the back. "We'll find you a hair and makeup artist." She lifted Esther's hand and studied her skin. "After the first series of treatments, you'll want a mehndi artist as well."

"Treatments?"

Parisa waved. "You learn more later today. Your group will have a meal and then Hegai will explain what you need to do." Parisa brushed Esther's hair away from her face and grinned. "A braid is the extent of my ability. Jasmine will take you to the courtyard. She has a good head on her shoulders. Be sure to use her wisely." With that compliment, Parisa disappeared into a different room. Esther waited a moment, but it didn't seem as though the other woman were coming back. Esther returned to the bedroom. Sun streamed through stained glass windows spilling color across the straightened bed. The room was empty. She opened a long window. Far below, fruit trees reached toward the bright blue sky with their bare branches.

"It won't always be quiet." Jasmine stepped beside Esther. "Especially once the girls and their companions find the gardens."

"Do all of us have a companion?"

"Most share."

"How many do you work with?"

"Oh, you are my only charge. I will be able to help with your other maidens."

"Esme and Parisa?"

"There will be a few more. We have room for seven. I want to acquire a teacher. I have asked Master Oonen. He is male, and as such is not permitted. He has no desire to take the order of the Eunuchs." Jasmine smirked. "He does enjoy his women. He may recommend someone."

"I have a teacher here in Shushan. Will I be able to visit with him?"

"He is not permitted to enter the women's compound, but there is a porch beside the gates. I will ask permission for you to meet with him there."

"I would appreciate that." Esther tilted her head. "Why have I received so much favor?"

"Favor is not something to question. You have an air about you that pleases. Yes, you are beautiful, but so are others. Hegai sees more in you."

"I am grateful for his blessing."

Jasmine grinned. "As are we. This wing is luscious. I will enjoy our year."

"Year?" Esther started.

"At least. You have a year of processes and rituals. When you are ready, you will be on the list to visit the king. After your stay with him, you move to the concubine's house."

"When can I go home?"

"You are the kings. Your home is with him now. Your fate is that of queen or concubine."

Esther looked out across the garden through the open window. A cold breeze blew into the room, causing her scarf to flutter. "I will be queen."

Jasmine's smile widened and she gave her a quick

hug. "I believe even Queen Mother Atossa will approve of you. She was not quite so fond of Vashti."

"Did you know the one who died?"

"She was beautiful as a sunrise, but not bright. She did not give notice to servants and companions."

"King Xerxes really had her killed?"

At this, Jasmine frowned, and her features darkened. "Never forget, life and death are in the hands of the king. Never give him reason to question your obedience or doubt your loyalty."

A cloud passed over the sun and a sudden gloom fell through the garden into her room. Esther shook it off, because a moment later, the sun brightened.

Jasmine perked. "You said you had a teacher living in Shushan. What is his name?"

"Mordecai."

***

Jasmine led Esther from the suite of rooms in the royal palace to the chamber beside Apadana where an assortment of benches, chairs, and stools were arranged on one side of a pond with a fountain. Esther recognized some of the girls from the previous day. Jasmine made sure she was settled.

"I will see you later. Be sure to remember any questions you have. I will enquire."

Esther was about to ask Jasmine to stay when she noticed none of the other maidens remained. She smiled.

"The great king, king of kings, Xerxes welcomes you," Hegai walked through the room, his voice projecting so all the women could hear.

Esther glanced around her group of thirty or so candidates. Beautiful young women from various walks of life. A few seemed uncomfortable in the linen clothes they wore. Some held back tears while others let their tears flow freely.

"Our first task will be your assessment." Hegai continued. He gazed on each of them, meeting their eyes.

Esther appreciated his direct gaze. His dark eyes were determined, and yet compassionate. It seemed he smiled at her and she gave a slight nod.

"You must be honest with me. The king requires virgins. He wants what no other man has touched. If you suspect you may be pregnant, inform us now. We can arrange your return. If you are found pregnant a few months from now, you and your child will be destroyed as an affront to his majesty."

A girl sitting on a wool blanket started to cry. By a shake of his head, Hegai had her removed. Esther never saw her again.

"Very well." Hegai walked the room. "Your assessment will determine the treatments you receive. Three times a week you will bathe with oil. Your diet will maximize the quality of your hair, skin, and nails. You will have a regimen of cosmetics determined by your companions. Every day, you must walk to enjoy the compound. Always you must be guarded. Do not leave the women's quarters."

"Will there be more than just walking for us to do?" One of the young ladies lounging behind Esther asked.

Hegai did not seem perturbed by the interruption. "Your king appreciates an active mind and body. Courses for learning new crafts and artisan skills will be available to you. You will want to learn dance and games that can be played during a feast. Learn musical instruments or even sing. Your companions will record what you would like to do." Hegai clapped and two servants appeared. "Bethryn and Rodon will guide you to the gardens. Walk the grounds to familiarize yourselves and then a light luncheon will be served. I will speak with your companions and prepare them for what they are to do for you."

One of the women watched fearfully as others stood and started to wander. She stood up hesitantly as the others moved toward double doors leading out of the large meeting room. Esther moved towards her instead of the doors.

"Are you well?" She asked in the common Persian language.

The girl blinked but did not respond.

Esther smiled gently. The woman had lighter skin and brown eyes. She had to be from one of the more northern regions. She tried an Indian language. "It's hard when you don't understand others." She guessed well.

The woman sobbed. "You understand my language?"

"A little. You will have to teach me more than I already know."

Hegai stepped beside them. "Is there a problem?"

"Oh, no. We have figured out how to communicate. May I share with her what you have told us today?"

Hegai nodded. "I hoped you would be able to assist her. She must learn our common tongue." He moved away.

Esther linked arms with the woman. "My name is Esther." She reverted to the Indian language.

"I have not heard a voice I understand since I arrived in this cursed place."

"You do not want to be here?"

"What am I supposed to do? I have no chance of becoming queen. I have seen Queen Vashti. I am nothing like her."

"None of us can be. They seem to want us to build a life for ourselves here."

"What do you mean?"

"There is a year of preparations. I do not yet understand the extent. We have opportunities to learn as well."

"Is that what the tall black man said?"

"His name is Hegai. He prescribes the treatments we are to receive and opportunities for learning." Esther grinned. "Your first task will be to learn the common tongue."

They walked into the garden. Though the air was chill, the bright sun rising higher made things comfortable. They walked together in the light. "What is your name?" Esther asked her.

"Idaljeb. It comes to me from my grandmother. Most people call me Ida."

"An elegant name. Did it take many days for you to travel here?"

She grimaced. "I still have bruises. They dumped me in a bath almost when I arrived." She giggled. "Not that I complained. The oils smell far better than I did."

They continued to chat as they wandered through shaped trees that still had leaves. More bare branches marked the winter season. Ida teased Esther's pronunciation of some words, and Esther taught names of things they passed. Ringing bells announced the meal.

"There are olives, dates, I'm not sure about this one." Esther picked up a flower on the tray. It smelled sweet. "Do you think it is edible?" She glanced at Ida who giggled with a shrug.

"This is cheese." Ida swept her finger through a creamy looking sauce.

Someone else at the table frowned at her. Esther glanced down. "Guess we should not do that." She turned the large circular tray. "Oh, walnuts and almonds."

After the meal, a companion led Ida to the bathing house for the newer portion of the women's quarters. Esther wandered around, passing through an arched opening in a wall to another garden. If her instincts were correct, the uphill climb should lead her to the gardens outside her suite. With winter upon them, no flowers bloomed in the garden boxes set against the walls of the palace. Trees groomed in a variety of shapes were set across the lawn. She stopped when she noticed the building added to the garden. It was round, almost twice her height, with a door. Some sort of thin material spread across the pillars. She couldn't see through the material, but it allowed light inside. Esther pulled the door to go inside. A green sofa provided a place for her to sit. Cleo would do well in the space.

Esther used her key to enter the palace. She intended to find a quiet place to rest, but Jasmine saw her on the stairs.

"There you are." Jasmine hurried to her side. "Mistress Khepri is waiting for you. She has received oils and wants to begin treatments."

"Treatments?"

Jasmine smiled. "Hot baths. I think you will be pleased."

***

Steam wafted from the copper tub filled with water.

Khepri poured myrrh from her vial and added handfuls of eucalyptus cuttings. At first, the heat of the water stung, and then enveloped her in its warmth. Khepri placed a folded towel on the edge of the tub. "Lay your head here."

Esther rested against the side of the tub with her eyes closed as Khepri brushed through her hair. The heady smell of myrrh mingled with other oils she used to massage Esther's scalp and then condition her hair.

"It is a pretty color, although we could lighten it with a little turmeric." She wrapped a towel around her hair and then pinned it in place.

"It will turn gray soon enough. I'd rather keep my natural color."

"As you wish." Khepri accepted a small tub from two servants. "Sit up and hold your arms out." She pulled a wrap of linen soaked in oils. She wiped as much of the excess as she could before wrapping each of Esther's arms.

"What is this?"

"The mixture of frankincense and myrrh will soften your skin and make it supple to touch and see. Time to stand." Once Esther followed directions, she had her hold one end of a wide strip of linen. "Now, if you'll turn slowly, I think this will work. We can wrap your torso here and move you to the lounge after."

Esther did as told, and Khepri was able to secure the linen at her waist. She rang a bell and two men entered. Esther gasped. "I am not dressed."

Khepri laughed. "They are eunuchs. Their desire is for political power. By serving you, if you become queen, they will in turn be served. Now, keep your arms out straight and hold them firm."

One on either side of the tub placed a hand at her armpit and against her back. They lifted her easily and high enough she didn't have to move her legs to keep from hitting the sides of the tub. Heat drove into her face and it was all she could do not to burst into tears. Khepri must have realized her distress because she brought a short skirt and allowed Esther to cover herself.

"The back is longer than the front. Bring it under you, as though you are wearing a diaper and tuck it in the front. We will still need to wrap your legs. Bedri and Halnif will help."

Esther appreciated the gesture and found it easier to lay on the formed mat, her torso and head elevated, as the men lifted her leg so Khepri could wrap it.

"How long do I stay wrapped like this?" It felt odd, and yet, the odor of the oils was pleasant.

"A few hours. We will keep the linens moist. Ah, music has arrived." Khepri motioned for the guests to use a far corner.

A pair of women stood in a corner of the room. The deeper sound of the barbat lute played into the higher pitch of the stringed surna. The music helped for a while. More servants brought fresh oil to rub on the linens to keep them moist, which eased the occasional urge to itch.

Still, time lagged. Jasmine came in, lounging against a pillow beside Esther's bed. "Every day there will be different treatments. Your skin is better than most. Living in Susa must help prevent the ridges caused by desert air. Some of the girls," she shook her head. "The stench they carry will take a month of oil baths to overcome. Khepri has obtained a generous amount of the oils for your use. We have a room where things can be stored."

"Is there enough for the others?" Esther could only turn her head to look at Jasmine.

Jasmine nodded. "Of course. You are well supplied, but no one will lack for their needs. In fact, Esme has been granted an afternoon in the royal kitchen. She attends one who prepares meals for Queen Mother Atossa. It is a great privilege. A handful of cooks have been granted access."

"Esme will need someone to translate for her. She only speaks Hebrew. What is the queen mother like? Will I meet her?"

"I hear she will walk through the women's compound sometime in the coming weeks. I believe she will search for someone more fitting to wed her son. She is not a woman to cross; after all, Xerxes is her son. Age is growing on her. She makes use of her chair more frequently."

"I pray she lives long and gets to see a new heir born to the king."

"A new heir? There is Darius."

"Even with what happened to Queen Vashti?"

Jasmine laughed. "I have little understanding of those sorts of intrigues. May Xerxes defy the gods and live forever."

Esther closed her eyes. "Have the other women started treatments like this?"

"Some have. They will rotate days, with one day off per week."

Khepri stood at Esther's feet. "We are ready to return to the bath."

Esther looked at Jasmine. "Have you met Khepri?"

Jasmine smiled at the other woman. "I have not, but I have heard she brings rare oils and spices with her."

Esther communicated Jasmine's words to Khepri. Khepri offered a bow. "There is an enclosed garden house. I have been granted permission to plant. Conditions can be made similar to what I knew in Egypt."

Esther shared the news. Jasmine's eyes shined with enthusiasm. "Wonderful. Let me know if you can use help. I enjoy working in the garden."

Bedri and Halnif returned. Khepri motioned for them to help Esther stand and then carry her to the copper tub once again filled with fresh steaming water.

Jasmine skipped after them. "I will fetch Parisa to the wardrobe. I think she plans to take measurements."

Removal of the linens felt lovely. Esther sighed as she lay back in the water. A loofah removed the oils without abrasing her skin. With only this first treatment, her skin felt smooth and silky. "A year of this? I shall be absolutely spoiled." She sighed.

Khepri laughed. "You expect a queen not to be spoiled? Here, use this, and we will return you to your rooms."

Esther accepted the light robe gratefully, covering up her nakedness. A button and belt secured it. "I can find my way."

Khepri frowned. "Are you sure? With the wings constructed quickly, hallways become more like a maze. I don't want to lose the person who can talk with me."

"I have a good sense of direction. I will see you later. Join us for the evening meal and we'll work on new words."

"After everything I've put you through, you would still invite me to join you for a meal?"

"Neither of us have a choice in being here. I would

rather do what I must to win the crown. I need your skills to accomplish that. Besides, you are worth knowing."

"Thank you. Yes, I will join you for dinner."

Chapter: A Start to Assessments

"**Master Hegai has** brought another maiden. Her specialty is cosmetics and hair." Jasmine entered Esther's suite with a young woman in tow.

Esther stopped moving the ribbon she used to play with Cleo. The kitten continued to twist the ribbon around her paws. "Salaam alaykum. I am Esther."

The woman nodded with enough enthusiasm to make her curly hair bounce around her head. "I am Banu."

Jasmine took Cleo to the window and gave her a small bowl with shredded bits of chicken and duck. "We have a room with a table and drawers for brushes and cosmetics. They built a small fireplace to heat an iron."

"I am eager to explore, but first, we should evaluate Mistress Esther's condition. A chair placed in full sun would be best."

Esther stood. "In the garden?"

"With others looking on?"

Jasmine led them into the main room. "There is a private deck above us." She led them past the fountain and up the far set of stairs.

Esther traced a finger across the image of the king's

face on a winged beast. "I have not explored this area."

Jasmine grinned. "We do not give you time to explore." The upper hall had a large doorway which opened onto a marble-floored deck. She moved a chair into full sun. "At least it is winter. In summer, I fear this space will be like fire during the day."

Banu rubbed her hands together. "Have a seat and let us look. We must start with the hair." She drew her hand through Esther's long tresses. "Your hair is thick and strong, but very rough." She glanced at Jasmine. "Have Et Tu flower added to her diet. It is from Egypt. Added in salads is best, a third serving three times a week. We will also need jojoba seeds. Crush them in olive oil for a hair mask. Add oatmeal for some texture. Twice a week for now, I think."

"Esme should prepare that?"

"The cook?"

Jasmine smiled. "She is a food artist."

Banu waved. "Tell her she may put the concoction in a fancy jar."

"She will, if you give her the idea."

Banu grinned as she considered bangs on Esther. "There are several cuts we can try. With the right nutrition, we could cut your hair up to your chin and it would grow back by the fall."

Esther felt her stomach drop even as she stiffened.

Banu patted her should. "I won't, I promise. We will need to tame this crop. Add some layers for shape. I think we can get you a wave."

Esther shivered at the thought of her hair being cut. "Is that necessary?"

"Braids, plaits, curls- they all form better and stay longer in the proper setting. I can start with something you will barely notice. For now, we'll use the treatments to make repairs." She took hold of Esther by the chin and tilted her head up and to the left and then the right. "Master Hegai said you didn't appear to have sun damage. You do have a flurry of freckles across your nose and cheeks. A vinegar scrub should keep those faded. Your forehead has space for a headdress. I will speak with... who is your wardrobe mistress?" She released Esther and stepped back.

"Parisa?"

"Ah, yes. She should be able to help. What about the oils mistress? She should be here."

Jasmine stood. "I will bring her."

Esther kept her hands in her lap though she was tempted to twist her hair and hide it away from Banu's eager hands. "Khepri does not speak the common tongue. I will speak with her about what is needed."

"We must help teach the common language to any of your maidens who do not know it." Banu pulled a pair of scissors from a bag. She placed her hand on Esther's shoulder. "Close your eyes. You won't fear as much." She made cuts as she continued her evaluation. "I think for now we do one cosmetic updo each week. We can use this time to play with colors. Once the repair treatments have concluded, we'll be able to do more."

Khepri joined them. "Greetings. What is happening?"

Esther made sure Banu's scissors were not near her hair before rising. "This is Banu, she will be working with us. Her expertise is hair and cosmetics."

"Wonderful," Khepri clapped her hands. She bowed toward Banu.

Esther translated for them.

"Do you have any storing of oils yet?" Banu asked as she put her tools in a linen pouch.

"Masters have been good to us. Would you like to see what we have?" She offered them a tour of the shelves in the wet room.

The group followed her back inside the suite of rooms. Esme joined them. Banu peered at Esther. "Are other young women brought to this area?" Banu stared.

"No, this is my suite of rooms. I have been honored."

The wet room was down another corridor. Khepri led them to storage shelves. "Myrrh is a healing oil. Its scent is a bit dark, but we can add different oils as they become available." Khepri pulled a jar from the open shelving on the wall above the tub. "I think these symbols must be Sanskrit. They are not hieroglyphs." She opened the lid and waved her hand to smell. "Ah, lavender. This is good for rest and beauty."

"May I smell?" Esther reached for the jar. She touched one of the bracelets Khepri wore. "These are beautiful."

She held the jar allowing Esther to smell. Esther moved so Esme and Jasmine could smell as well. Banu toyed with her brushes in a different corner of the bathing room. Khepri jangled the bracelets on her arm. "The women of my village made these and gave them to me when I decided to follow Amon to Persia to study the art of oil preparations."

"Did your mother make one of them."

"This," Khepri said, lifting her other arm with only two bracelets. "Mother made the red. She cut each bead from the Kamah tree and rolled them in oil for twenty-one days." The reddish hue of the beads seemed to glitter in the light coming into the room from its many high windows.

"Is that a black oil?" Esther pointed at a clear bottle.

"Ground pumice. It is given to us by the gods of the volcano. It has no scent but is used to scrub and smooth skin. This, I am sure, you will like." She lifted a different jar. When she took the lid off, they could all smell rose.

Esme perked up. "I think they are growing those in the winter house."

Esther interpreted for Khepri, then added, "I adore rose blooms. Bring some if you can." Esther closed her eyes and inhaled. "Can we mix rose with myrrh?"

Khepri wrinkled her nose. "Not a good match. They will both try to overwhelm the other."

"Banu," Esther called to the other woman. "What of hair? Is there an oil that is good to process hair?"

She joined them. "Rosemary, and a variety of mint. Ask if there is rosemary or mint oil on the shelf."

"Khepri?" Esther asked by repeating Banu's words.

Khepri studied the contents of the shelf and touched one of the small bottles. "Mint is here. Notice the greenish cast to the bottle." Khepri smiled at Banu. "Rosemary we will have to make. There is a greenhouse for the main kitchens?"

Esther repeated for the others. Esme raised her hand. "There is a winter house and a greenhouse. I can look for the rosemary. How much would you need?"

"About two pounds," Khepri answered once Esther repeated the question. "It is a rich oil and should meld well with an olive oil base."

"Ah, darling, here you are." Parisa swept into the room holding her arms wide. "I have stolen Mistress Gaezel from the lower hall. She will take measurements and we shall plan your wardrobe."

Esther swallowed. "You have already filled the wardrobe."

"My dear girl, there is much more. Spring will be here. There will be parties and feasts. A faction of the women's court will be taken to the summer grounds. Beauty treatments continue." She paused to clasp her hands to her chest. "Wouldn't it be lovely if we were chosen to go?"

"Would I meet the king sooner?"

"Oh, no, dear. It's as though he enjoys the thought of them being there. The women who are scheduled will go, of course. They will be brought back to the harem the next day." She clapped her hands. "Are we ready? I don't want to give Mistress Gaezel reason to head in a different direction."

Esther glanced at Jasmine.

"I can reschedule Banu's hair treatment. If you don't mind, we can work on a list of educational pursuits."

When they returned to the suite of rooms, Esther and Parisa went into the wardrobe rooms. Cushioned chairs had been moved into the space along with a writing table and a stool covered with green material. Mistress Gaezel finished writing on a scroll, then stood. She was tall and willowy, with her hair pulled back in thick ties. A scar of puckered skin marred her cheek. Her eyes were a rich color of hazel. She held up a cream-colored handful of fabric. When Parisa took it from her, Esther could see a short shift. It had no sleeves and would likely sit above her knees. Parisa snapped her fingers. "Now is not the time to daydream. Remove what you have on so we can get you into this."

Esther did as directed. The shift covered her, barely. Chill air made her shiver.

Jasmine crossed the room. "I'll get a little fire going in the next room. Warm the air."

Mistress Gaezel reached into her bag and brought out a strip of fabric. "Each item must have a precise measurement," she explained. "I have marked this at regular intervals, and it helps me make clothes that fit you perfectly." She laid other items on the table. They looked like cushions in a variety of shapes and sizes. "You need a coat." She picked one of the cushions and crossed to Esther. "This fills in the shoulders," she placed the cushion on Esther's shoulder then took a measurement. "We need the other arm." She moved the cushion. "Now stretch your arm forward. You want to be able to move."

She took every measure conceivable. Several jackets were to be short, to her waist. One must be expecting to be a long cape with a wide start. She measured her feet and ankles, her ears, and the depth of her forehead.

The cat jumped into Esther's lap, causing Mistress Gaezel to step back. "What is this creature?"

"Oh, she's harmless. I couldn't leave her at home with no one to care for her." The cat settled on Esther's lap. Mistress Gaezel went to measure her forearm for gloves, but the kitten reached for the measuring tool. She batted at the end swinging near her head. The women laughed. Mistress Gaezel held the ribbon higher. The kitten fell backward, making them laugh harder. Mistress Gaezel's eyes sparkled. "We best get back to work."

"I will remove the distraction," Jasmine said as she scooped up the kitten, holding it close.

Mistress Gaezel nodded. "I have seen a few of the Grecian relics brought back from the wars." She worked a measurement from shoulder to opposite waist. "They embellish with ribbons of lace. You have the figure for such a look. It has a high skirt, starting under the breasts, but very little flow. Here, hold this." She indicated for Esther to hold the measuring tool. It didn't quite reach the floor. Esther leaned over to look. "Keep straight," Mistress Gaezel corrected. She pulled another piece of fabric, cut it to the length she wanted, and then hurriedly sewed it to the longer piece. Before long, the last of the measurements were taken. Mistress Gaezel and Parisa disappeared in the other room. Esther rolled her eyes at Jasmine. "I feel as though I need a nap, or one of those hot baths. I don't think I've ever contorted my body in such a way."

Jasmine giggled. "What sort of dress starts at the back of your head and goes to the floor?"

Esther glanced at the other room but didn't see anyone. "She may create as she will, but I wear as I will."

Jasmine nodded. "I hope Parisa understands your style."

"Good afternoon," Esme interrupted as she entered. "I thought you might enjoy something refreshing." She carried a round tray with a teapot and several cups. There were also small biscuits on a plate and a pile of blue fruits. She placed the tray on the table. "I found the fruit in the winter house. I think you will enjoy it's flavor."

"I'm cold. Let me grab a robe, and then we can enjoy refreshments." Esther rubbed her arms. She turned, but Jasmine already stood nearby with a warmer wrap. "Blessings upon you," Esther said as she grabbed the robe and put it on. They sat around the table and ate from the bowl of berries.

"They are sweet. Not too juicy, but look," Esme squeezed one and her fingers became stained with blue.

Jasmine's eyes widened. "Will it do that to us on the inside?"

Esther grinned. "Your teeth don't look blue, so I think we are good."

"You need to decide on some activities. How would you like to learn archery?" Jasmine sipped hot tea.

"Bow and arrows?" Esther repeated for Esme. "Does that mean we could learn to use a sword as well? I have always wanted to try."

"I don't see why not. Anything less strenuous you would like to try?"

"My teacher taught me to read and write."

"Oh, my goodness, I nearly forgot." Esme jumped to her feet. "I'll be right back." She ran from the room.

"What was that about?" Jasmine watched her go.

"She said she forgot something and would be right back."

"Odd. I hope nothing bad has happened. I heard something about pottery. They have all sorts of musical instrument trainers. Even someone for singing."

Esther grinned. "Hopefully, there will be discernment for choosing who will sing."

Jasmine chuckled. "I know I wouldn't be any good."

"Me neither, but I think I would like to learn to flute."

***

Mordecai wandered along the wall leading to the King's Gate. His walking stick of ash helped him with the sharp incline to the palace. The pavement passed through a wide passageway with two halls and two porticoes each with two columns. Once through the passageway, he continued, following the sharp right turn. Stone rose high on one side of the walkway. From the other side, he looked across the plain of Susa. On a clear day, sunlight would sparkle across waters of the Tigris. Today was not a sunny day. As he neared the gates, the road crossed a brick causeway. Water gurgled in pools with fountains lining the stairs into the gatehouse.

"Shalom," Chanoch greeted as Mordecai reached the lower gate.

"Shalom aleichem," he replied.

"Shavua Tov?"

Mordecai grimaced. "My week would be better if I knew how Hadassah fairs."

Chanoch tapped the silver knob of his spear on the rock. "Hm, there is the outer courtyard of the Women's compound. If by chance you meet a servant for Esther, you may learn of her condition and perils."

Mordecai tried to see beyond the gatehouse, but the structures of the palace and Apadana blocked his view. Chanoch invited him through the gatehouse. A lane opened to the left. "Follow this. You will go past the Apadana. Go around to the back of the tower and you will see the high walls of the women's quarters. Follow the walk along the wall until you reach the open courtyard. The gates are wide, and servants pass through frequently. May YHWH guide your steps. Yasher kiach."

Mordecai gripped forearms with his friend. "Aleichem Shalom." He continued with the directions across the impressive palace and its surrounding royal city. Apadana dominated the block. Pillars rose like sentinels topped with bulls hardy enough to carry the load of the roof. Feeling dwarfed, he gazed through long windows. Indoors, the pillars were covered with royal blue. He could just make out purple drapes. Somewhere within, a bell rang. A symphony of lutes and tanburs with their three strings answered the bell. In the corner passing the Apadana, a small temple had been built to the god Mithra. From one of the arched openings, he spied a bowl filled with flames. Gray smoke rose from the fire, smelling of rosemary and cedar. He hurried past as the evidence of idol worship turned his stomach. A little further and he reached the high wall surrounding the women's complex.

Mordecai followed the path beside the wall. He passed periodic narrow windows. There were fountains, arches draped with colorful flowers and greenery, and long, low planters filled with what appeared to be herbs. Finally, at the third corner, he walked into a large open courtyard. Ahead of him were eight blue pillars topped with golden scrolls. Black iron gates filled the spaces between the pillars. The courtyard on this side of the gates was laid with blue square tiles surrounded by vivid green grass. What he could see of the other side was an opulent two-story plaza supported with more columns around a large pool with a tiered fountain. Colorful lounges and tables surrounded the pool. There were women, though he could not tell if any were Hadassah.

The third gate was open, and servants went back and forth. Mordecai sat on a step and considered what to do next. A few moments of ponderings, and then he realized someone watched him. A woman with black straight hair and thick bangs cut even with her eyebrows studied him. She bit her lip, tilted her head one direction, and then the other direction. She finally stepped closer as though she had made a decision.

"Are you Mordecai?"

He stood, excitement making his fingers itch. "Why would you ask that?"

"You look like him, I think. I mean, you look like the man she drew."

"Who drew?"

"Esther. She is my charge. Well, I mean, I cook for her. It is for that reason I have passed this way. We have permission to get fresh vegetables from the springhouse."

Mordecai blinked. Was it possible? Of course, it was, here was the proof. "I am Mordecai. She has told you about me?"

The woman's smile widened. "You are her teacher. I guess, since her parents died, she looks on you more like family."

"As do I. I feel as though I raised her once her parents were gone. I know I am not permitted to see her, leastwise not until she has been to the king. Would it be possible to meet you here sometimes? To get updates on her? Perhaps send a note through you?"

"I am happy to help. I mean, of course, Jasmine would be the better person. She's a companion. She spends more time with Esther and can share more."

"Would you talk with her about it?" Mordecai leaned in. "I will wait here every day to hear news of Had… of Esther." He pulled a thin scroll wrapped in deep red fabric. "Would you give her this? For her doorpost."

Esme's eyes widened. "A Mezuza?"

"The words of YHWH are a talisman of hope and

courage. My hope is she will use what she has learned of writing and send me a note."

The woman nodded. "I will speak with her tonight."

"What is your name?"

"Esme."

"Thank you, Esme. I appreciate your help, and your watch care over Esther. Shalom."

She nodded. "Shalom Aleichem." She walked away.

Mordecai grinned.

***

"I spoke with someone who knows you," Esme exclaimed when she returned.

Esther tilted her head. "Who? Where?"

Esme pointed at the basket of greens she placed on a table. "I went to the winter house for fresh vegetables. I recognized him from your drawing. The man you said is your teacher. What was his name, Mordecai?"

Esther's heart leapt. "Mordecai? Where did you see him?"

"He was wandering in the open courtyard. How fortuitous I saw him."

"Is he still there? Oh, I would not be permitted to speak to him."

Esme placed her other hand on Esther's arm. "Not at this time, but someday you will be. Until that time, we plan to communicate for you. He gives you this."

Esther took the Mezuza from Esme. "It is a blessing you found him. Or he found you."

Esme pointed at the scroll. "Father Moses told our people to write His words where we would see them rising up and laying down."

Esther squeezed her hand around the relic. "This is

intended for a doorway. At the lower end of the hall, do you think? I could have Master Eldij carve a place for it."

"Did you want to write to him?"

"Oh, yes. Tonight. Ask Jasmine to bring parchment and ink." Esther directed as she placed the artifact on a table in the hallway of their suite.

Chapter: A new servant for Esther

"**You are an** irresponsible menace. You have no right touching my things."

"I touched nothing. You backed into the shelf and caused the vase to fall." A pale-skinned, red-haired young woman glared at the other women with her hands on her hips.

The other woman pushed her back. "How dare you suggest I would lie? I'll have you in a dungeon before an hour has passed."

Esther noticed the pale woman wore the mantle of a servant. Days turned to weeks, yet some of the young women did not settle into their new life gracefully. She hurried to where the candidate stood quivering in anger.

"Oh, my," Esther interjected. "There are few enough servants helping us. Allow me to take her."

The women glared. "And leave me without assistance?"

"Throwing her in the dungeon would leave you without assistance. What if I offer you a trade? I will accept responsibility for the servant. Bethryn is of the order of Eunuchs. I will send him to you, and he will find what you need in an assistant."

The woman's face cleared. "A Eunuch? They carry political clout. I can accomplish a great deal more with one of them than this palm worm." Her lip curled. "Send him to me." She turned with a dramatic tilt to her head and flounced into her room.

The pale worm blinked at Esther, her lip twitching. Esther swallowed the urge to giggle and motioned for the servant girl to follow her. "I take it, you have not been with her long."

The girl widened her eyes. "One has to be willing to learn."

"Are you a teacher?"

She nodded. "My name is Douika. I was placed with a priest. He noticed I had a mind for learning. It is by his hand I can write and read."

"Do you know languages?"

"Greek, Aryan, Latin, Celtic, Hebrew- I have had many opportunities."

Esther grinned. She switched to Latin. "Which language is your home language?"

"Ah, a fellow multilingual. I am from the northernmost regions," she pulled her red braid, "in case you couldn't tell. Celtic is my home language. I doubt Latin is yours."

"I grew up speaking Arabic and Hebrew."

"Are your parents a mix?"

"They died when I was a child. I was raised by my cousin."

"I don't know if my parents are alive or dead. I have no memory of them. Sometimes I dream of a green land, green as an emerald."

"I would love to see such a land." Esther walked to the guard at her doorway. "Good morning, Injon.

"Mistress Esther," he greeted with a bow and then swept the door open for her.

Douika stared. "You live in this section?"

"There are rooms for all of us. I will introduce you to the other young maidens who assist me." She turned to the soldier. "Would you be so kind as to locate Master Bethryn and ask him to attend to me? I have…" she glanced at Douika, "a challenging task for him?"

Douika sucked on her lips to keep from laughing.

"Jasmine is my companion. She will coordinate lessons, of which you will be in charge. Then there is Esme. Let her know what you like for your meals. She prepares for us."

"You eat together?"

"I hate to eat alone. Khepri will appreciate your knowledge of languages. She speaks Egyptian."

"Who are the others?"

"Parisa." Esther glanced quickly around the empty common area of her wing. "I am still figuring her out. I think she is the oldest of us. Here, this room is available for you." Esther led her to a small room with a single door. The chamber had tiles of gray and green. The walls were green as well with printed leaves in various sizes. Gold corbels atop partial columns in each corner added a formal air to the room.

Douika gasped. "I am to live here? How is that possible?"

Esther grinned. "I ask myself that every day."

"I had a mat in the corner in Deligia's quarters. Is that my bed?" She stared at the mound on the floor piled with blankets and a cushion.

"Yes. And there will be space to hang a few garments. If you are to be my instructor, you will need to have appropriate clothes."

"I have never turned down an opportunity for clothes."

"Parisa helps. Now, let me show you the rest of the space."

Esther guided Douika through the series of rooms where more and more clothes hung from hooks in the wall. "This is a room you may use as needed." Esther showed her how to pull a cord to make the toilet function.

"What is the water for?"

"My father-cousin taught me cleanliness. Washing hands and face is a daily ritual."

"What manner of things do you expect me to be able to teach you?"

"I will need something to occupy my time when not being harassed with oil baths and other beauty regiments."

Douika peered at Esther. "What do you think you will need for the palace that you don't already have?"

"You ask a good question." She thought for a moment. "The king appreciates music and I never learned to play or sing. Is that something I could learn in a year?"

"I can find what resources are available." Douika shrugged.

"We ask Hegai who will have the charge of that."

"Master Hegai? He is outside my capability. I could never ask of him."

Esther smiled. "We talked a few times. I will find out."

They heard a door closing from the bottom of the stairs. A few moments later, Esme arrived.

Esther called her to join them. "We have acquired

our teacher."

"That is wonderful!" Esme exclaimed.

Esther introduced them. "This is Esme. Esme, this is Douika. She will be our teacher. Instructor. Something helpful."

Douika grinned. "We figure it out together." She nodded at Esme. "Do you need help? I have a little knowledge of cooking, but I can always learn more."

"Go with her, I will see you later." She turned to Esme. "I have prepared a note for Mordecai, would you take it to him?"

She nodded. "He said he would wait to hear news from you."

"Wonderful." She had taken about five steps toward her room, when she paused and turned back to the other two women. "I don't think I have any more parchment or ink."

"I have a sheet of rice paper," Douika offered.

Esme indicated she should join them. "I saw hyacinth flowers drying. They may be good for blue ink."

Esther's smile widened. "I will follow you."

The kitchen area was down another set of steps. The room was about the size of a servant's sleeping quarters, except on the far wall was a door opening into a patio and garden area. The feel of winter could be seen in the dead plants, but an oven with warming bricks gave off heat to combat the cold. They found the hyacinth flowers. "Who set these here to dry?" There was a mound, as though someone cut them before they would be of no good and plopped them on a table near the kitchen.

Esme shrugged. "Gardeners. Take some back with

us. Khepri can help make the ink, she should have an oil."

Esther took several handfuls and placed them in her bag. "When will you go to the other kitchen?"

"This afternoon. I will find Mordecai and give him your note."

"You have more reason to travel between the women's quarters and the main palace. Are you comfortable meeting with him?"

Esme smiled. "He is kind. What else may I share with him?"

"All news is good. See if he will share news with us as well. There is little we get to hear inside these walls." Esther looked down. Esme hadn't had as much freedom. "I think I will take a walk in the garden."

She hadn't gone far when she recognized one of the candidates. Ida sat on a hard bench staring at the twisted branches of a rose bush whose leaves had fallen. "Winter leaves everything cold and dead," she said without turning to look at Esther.

"It won't always be that way. The season will turn."

Ida sighed. "Will it? I don't see any turning."

Esther sat beside her. "We are not used to our new circumstance."

"Should we not be enemies?"

Esther smiled. "We have as much control over the king's choice as we do in our being here. What purpose would there be in enmity between us?"

Ida relaxed. "It is hard to know what we should be."

"Find something to occupy your time and mind for when you are not in treatments. What did you do with your time before coming to Shushan?"

She contemplated her fingers. "They will not let me

craft baskets."

"Whyever not?"

"It is a menial job."

"Is it? Artisans are not menial. What materials do you use to build baskets?"

She shrugged. "I've used reeds dried from river grass. Bits of fabric. Beads."

"Speak with your companion. Supplies can be found. You could teach some of us."

Ida's face brightened. "Is it possible?" She glanced around. "I am not sure where my companion has gone."

"What is her name?"

Ida tilted her head. "She never said."

"Learn that as soon as you may. A person's name is their identity. They are here to help us. We should let them have an identity."

"I never thought of that. She is a kind woman making sure we are comfortable in our rooms."

Sometime later, along, Esther wandered the path of the labyrinth considering her conversation with Ida. What had she done with her time up till now? Life with Mordecai had been comfortable. Learning languages and listening in the marketplace was her common pursuit. She hadn't been interested in clothes or gossiping in town square. The house servant took care of laundering needs and cooking each week. She tried teaching children, but too often her attention drifted.

Here, languages helped others. Being able to read moods and intent provided opportunity. What could she accomplish as queen?

She spun around as she reached the inner section, then continued along the path moving outward. It was wrong to desire the position of queen. Much more likely, she would become a member of King Xerxes' harem. That did not bear thinking.

She pushed negative thoughts from her mind and focused on her feet. The leather boots had been waterproofed, so her feet remained dry though the path was damp. Green bushes cut like square boxes guided her way. She couldn't see the end, could only trust her path was leading her where she should go. The thought encouraged.

Chapter: Palace Life

Mordecai waited the next morning, sitting on a low wall around a fountain. Splashes of cold water kept him alert. He was soon rewarded, standing as he noticed the small woman exiting the women's compound. "Shalom." His smile widened as she nodded.

"Shalom, Master Mordecai. Your friend, Esther, sends blessings. I am heading towards the kitchens. Would you like to walk with me?"

"I am pleased to accompany you. How is Esther?"

"She is a bright star among the heavens. Her knowledge of languages helps many. I do not think they expected to collect women who don't speak Persian."

"Keeps her in the know, which I am sure she appreciates. Would it be permitted to give you something else for her?"

Esme shrugged. "I have not heard we cannot do so."

Mordecai pulled a beaded necklace and a small scroll. "Thank you."

Esme dug into her bag, found a small pouch, and put the items in it. They arrived at the kitchen compound. A tall, slender woman greeted Esme and then looked at Mordecai.

He nodded. "Shalom."

"Shalom." She spoke Hebrew. "I am Solique. Are you with Esme?"

"She is my connection with my…" he hesitated. "My former student who now resides in the women's quarter."

"Ah." She nodded. "You may be of assistance." She turned with the expectation of Esme and Mordecai following her. They went through the yard to a building of mostly glass. "This is the green house." Solique led them to a patch of ground with a scattering of small leaves breaking through the dirt. "A caravan brought Et Tu flowers. They grow very slow." Solique handed Esme a coconut. "The oil of this added to lavender will soften hair. Have one of the eunuchs break it open. You can also use the meat in some recipes."

"How may I be of assistance?" Mordecai asked, watching Solique. Though not young, her smooth skin complimented her dark hair pulled back in a simple bun. She had a kind face with a beauty mark beside her nose.

"Khepri, the oils mistress, asks for rosemary. About two pounds." She handed Mordecai a curved blade with a wooden handle. "Would you cut for us and carry the basket to the gate? Esme will take it the rest of the way."

"I am pleased to assist." He nodded. Beyond the green house was a row of rosemary shrubs. Once the basket was filled, he and Esme returned to the courtyard by the women's quarters.

***

Esme found Esther sitting on a balcony as she watched a pair of squirrels chase each other through the trees. "Mistress."

Esther turned. "Shalom."

Esther's greeting made Esme smile wider. "Shalom. I have been visiting with your teacher, Master Mordecai. Solique used him to cut fresh rosemary. I delivered the basket to Khepri." She drew something from her bag. "He also sends this."

Esther accepted the pouch. "Thank you."

"He seems keen on knowing your business."

"Master Mordecai is a sharp advisor. Whether we gain the crown or move into King Xerxes' harem, we need an advisor."

"I am sorry you are unable to talk with him in person at this time."

"It would not be worth the risk. I trust you to be our liaison if you have no caution against it."

Esme lowered her head. "I am honored by your trust. What should I say to him?"

"Be free with our news. He will not be impertinent."

Jasmine stuck her head through the opening. "There is an archery lesson on the main lawn of the garden. Would you like to join or watch?"

Esther jumped to her feet. "Oh, yes, I want to give it a try."

Esme stood. "I will see if Khepri needs help extracting oil from the rosemary."

Esther and Jasmine went to the designated area. A crowd of young ladies gathered. It wasn't until Esther noticed a tall woman with gray hair, she realized why so many had come. "It is Queen Mother Atossa."

A small circle of guards kept everyone at a distance and allowed Atossa to move through the crowd easily. She wore a gown of deep burgundy that highlighted the silvery-gray shimmer of her hair in the sunlight. The crown of gold with burgundy jewels marked her identity.

Jasmine stepped behind Esther as Atossa approached them. Esther bowed.

The queen nodded. "Have you used a bow?"

Esther lifted the wooden weapon. "This is my first attempt."

Atossa reached toward a guard who handed her his bow. She stepped beside Esther. The guard took position behind them. The crowd of ladies tried to position themselves to see through the men.

"Position your hands." Atossa demonstrated and then waited for Esther to mimic her. Atossa nodded and continued. "Pull this arm back. Watch your hand when you place your arrow to release. The sinews will hurt if they snap your hand."

Esther breathed then pulled back and let the sinew go. She could feel the force of it. "I need an arrow."

Atossa nodded, and someone handed Esther an arrow with a light point. Atossa set the shaft, raised her bow and fired an arrow. It sailed up and then arched toward the earth, where it stuck in a mound of hay. Esther copied her movements. The twang of the string was not as smooth, nor did her arrow travel as far, but Esther couldn't keep herself from grinning. "I shot an arrow."

"Practice will benefit you." Atossa handed her bow to a guard. Another went to retrieve her arrow.

Esther watched them leave, crossing the field. Most of the young ladies followed, but a few stayed to watch her.

Jasmine returned to her side. "You receive great honor."

"I think I need to go sit in the garden." The two of them went a different direction from the queen mother and her entourage. Esther headed for the cage house

Master Eldij built for Cleo.

***

"Mistress Esther," Hegai greeted.

Esther felt her cheeks heat, caught sitting on the ground inside as she teased Tanzia with a ribbon. The cat jumped into a box to hide from the stranger. "I am sorry, I was playing with her."

Hegai smiled. "You have nothing to apologize for. The king wishes to transport a group to Persepolis. You and your maidens have been selected to attend, if it pleases you."

Esther grinned. "I would love to travel."

He nodded. "Very well. Inform your maidens to be ready to leave in five days."

What more could this day bring? Esther couldn't find Jasmine, so she sat on a comfortable bench beneath an apple tree. Persepolis? Mordecai had gone, but she'd never been permitted to go with him. They weren't likely to allow much exploring, but she'd see something, wouldn't she?

A woman plopped onto the bench beside her, pulling Esther from her musings.

"Help me pick."

Esther stared at the woman. She'd seen her on occasion but had never talked with her. Her name was Yongisse. "I am not sure how I can help."

The woman grasped her hand. "Everyone claims you have exquisite taste."

"I do not know why anyone would say so. I am local, but my tastes are simple." Esther studied the woman. Yongisse' eyes were large. Her skin was the color of honey, balanced with dark silky hair. "You are very beautiful. What do you want?"

"Jewels and gems," she replied quickly.

Esther raised a brow. "Hegai can get them for you."

"Would I wear my hair up or down?"

"What does your hair artist recommend?"

"She wants to do a design of scrolls caught up with feathers. Do you think the king prefers fancy?"

Esther shrugged. "When I saw Queen Vashti, she had hair piled high." She used her hands to demonstrate.

Yongisse noticed one of the henna artists walking across the lawn. "Oh, I want to engage her services." She left with no further conversation.

Esther shook her head. "No doubt the coffers can adorn all of us. Is that to be payment for stealing our futures?"

Esme took Yongisse' seat and Esther repeated herself in Hebrew.

Esme nodded. "If it was to be the sparkle of gems that turns a king's head, we would be finished with this competition already."

"What attends a king's attention?" Esther chuckled. "Especially this one. How many women has he had thus far? How many more will he demand if none of us satisfy whatever it is he seeks?"

Esme smiled. "He'll need to send women to other palaces. There is little room remaining in Shushan."

Jasmine joined them. "A seamstress from Egypt is visiting. I secured her services. Parisa may appreciate working with someone from a different region."

"I have plenty in my wardrobe."

"She brings a renewed style." Jasmine sent Esther a sidelong glance. "And then there is always news. You can learn of Egypt."

Esther straightened. "I have news of my own."

Esme tilted her head. "What is it?"

Jasmine smiled. "Do you mean the queen?"

"Oh, no. Master Hegai visited. We are going to Persepolis for the summer." She repeated her news for Esme. Both women looked at each other, and then squealed.

"Of course, now we really need the services of the seamstress. You shall have a splendid wardrobe." Jasmine grabbed Esther's hand and pulled her to her feet. "We go now."

96

Chapter: The Great City of Persepolis

"I thought Susa extensive in size." Esther shook her head as she gazed across the great city. They entered the palace complex through the Gate of All Nations. Two monumental statues of bulls flanked the gate, meant to ward off evil but Esther still felt a chill of something shivering her back. They followed a winding road to the women's quarters. The whole of it was smaller than Shushan, yet she had been provided with the best suite.

"Come away from the balcony. The sun will damage your skin." Khepri waved Esther from the outdoors. When you travel, you do so with an umbrella. I arranged an audience of tattoo artists. The House of Assi produces the best. Hegai gives permission for you to select one to join us."

"Where do we meet them?"

"At the House of Assi. Hegai arranged transport." Jasmine's eyes glittered. "Your first trip in a carry cart."

"The curtains will be drawn so none can see you." Khepri assured Esther.

The cart was like a small room with a cushioned chair and curtains for walls. A half door allowed her to walk into the cart. Jasmine waited for Esther to sit and then she provided a thin blanket to cover her. "Would you like a pillow at your back?"

Esther nodded and leaned forward. *Much more comfortable*, she thought once settled. Curtain clips were used to be certain no one would be able to see her, yet the material was light enough Esther could see shapes and shadows moving. Jasmine exited and closed the door. Esther was on her own. There was a wobble as they lifted her. She grabbed the arms of the chair.

It was an odd feeling, being lifted into the air. Everything seemed muffled. The cart rocked as the servants walked the street. She swallowed a queasy feel as she swayed. The ride lasted nearly an hour. Esther let the blanket fall to the ground. What breeze passed into the cart did not provide much refreshing. Eventually, they stopped. Esther closed her eyes and grabbed the arms of the chair against as the cart tilted to set it down. Her head still rocked when Jasmine pulled back a curtain. Esther nearly jumped out of the cart, eager to be free of it. "I will gladly walk back."

"You know it is not permitted."

Esther grinned. "I require us all to wear veils then I may walk, and you ride."

Jasmine shook her head. "What trouble would follow if we were found out? No, you get to enjoy the privilege of the cart."

Esther laughed, but had no retort. Jasmine waved to an older woman standing in a doorway. They crossed the yard and greeted her.

The old woman touched her forehead and leaned forward. "Blessings be upon you this day. Welcome to the House of Assi."

"We are honored to visit." Jasmine responded.

"I am Roya, mistress of Assi. We arranged for you to examine twelve of our most advanced artists."

"How much training do they receive?" Esther asked as they walked into the building.

"They start young, becoming specialized in cosmetics and ritual markings. If they demonstrate an aptitude in the basics, they learn how to make henna; how to cultivate it for a variety of purpose."

They turned into a long hallway. One side was arched openings overlooking a garden. Benches were placed throughout. A young woman sat at each bench.

Esther straightened her shoulders. How was she to choose someone? Would the new girl get along with the others? From the corner of her eye, she saw something move. She turned to look. Across the hall, in an open room, someone painted on a long piece of linen. She drew a curved line of blue then the angled petals of a flower in red. The artist was young, possibly only a year or two older than Esther. Her hair was covered in a white wrap and she wore the common brown gown of the others.

"Will this be fabric for a coat?" Esther stepped into the room.

The woman jumped and turned. "I did not realize anyone was there."

"I have come from the palace of King Xerxes to select a tattoo artist."

"Is that why they have gathered in the courtyard?" She motioned to the other students.

"I like your style." Esther tilted her head as she studied the images. "Do you feel prepared to be an artist?"

Her green eyes widened. "You want me to work in the king's palace?"

"My name is Esther. I am a candidate to be queen. To me has been granted seven maidens to help in the preparations. I am indeed blessed. There are six already. I lack Mehndi to complete the beautifying process."

The woman laughed, but then realized Esther meant to ask her. "I am Zareen. I am not a master artist. Those across the way, they are your options."

Esther sighed. "But I like your style. I think you will get along with us."

"Mistress Roya will not permit me to go."

"We ask, if you want to join us."

Zareen glanced at the fabric. "I had no choice in coming to this house."

"We have precious few options to ourselves, but that does not mean we are not meant for great things."

Zareen watched Esther for a moment before nodding. "I accept, if Mistress Roya permits."

She did. In less than an hour, Esther swayed in the carry cart, thankful Mistress Roya offered juice and fresh fruit before they departed the House of Assi. Zareen and Jasmine followed, though she could not see them.

***

The long building of the women's quarters was plain in the front, an opening that led to a courtyard and then rooms. Most of the rooms were meager, except for a wing added at the end. Esther opened a door to one of the bedrooms. "You share this with Douika. She is our teacher and speaks many languages."

Zareen gasped. "There is room for more than the two of us."

"Parisa, Jasmine, and Khepri have the room beside

this. Esme and Banu are the first room. My room is in the back."

They walked into the common area. Afternoon sun beat on the balcony. "It is a delightful space in the morning." Esther closed the curtain to block heat.

Khepri glided into the room. "This is our Mehndi artist?" She reached for Zareen, kissing her cheeks in a traditional Egyptian greeting.

"Of a sort," Zareen shrugged.

"I am the oils mistress. Solique of Shushan provided a basket of dried henna leaves. Do you know how to prepare a mixture?"

"We'll need to crush the leaves into a fine powder. Mix the paste with sugar, lemon juice, and a setting oil. Melaleuca or lavender, we can test what works best on Esther's skin. Or Eucalyptus oil if that is available. It provides a different sort of scent."

Khepri moved to Esther. "Your skin has no signs of disease or marring. The months of myrrh treatments has made you supple and smooth. We use other spices and ointments to enhance your beauty. What Mehndi should we introduce?"

"Typical tattoos are on the hands and feet. I like to use a darker color on the fingertips and lighten as I move closer to the wrists."

"Is there a way to remove it if I do not like it?"

Zareen nodded. "Salts are the best way to be rid of it."

"I look forward to learning more."

"Your next treatment is tomorrow." Khepri glanced at Zareen. "Is there enough time to mix a paste?"

"We can prepare everything and mix six hours ahead of time."

"We get what is needed in the morning. Treatments begin at the noon hour."

***

Time in Persepolis lagged. Unable to explore the foreign city or see anything beyond the women's quarters, Esther spent her time with her maidens learning games. Douika taught them all a rock toss around a curved shape she called a rune. Esme challenged them to make shapes of wood that spun.

"I cannot do this," Parisa exclaimed at another failed attempt to twist her fingers in order to get the rounded top spinning.

"Give us something else," Zareen laughed at her failed attempt.

Esme thought a moment. "There is a game my brothers enjoyed. We need to make something round and big enough to hold in our hands."

"Like what?"

Esme searched the room. "What if we roll the blanket and wrap it with a piece of fabric?"

They soon had something that could work. Parisa set a bottle on the floor across the room. Parisa stood with the ball in her hands.

"Toss it to knock down the bottle." Esme directed.

Parisa lunged but missed. The ball rolled harmlessly about halfway to the bottle.

Everyone had a turn, but it wasn't until Esme that the bottle got hit.

As the sun headed towards its western rest, Esther, Douika, and Banu went to the gardens. Before they cleared the trees, they heard a young woman shouting.

"I will not be treated this way. How am I to please the king in these circumstances? I demand another opportunity in Susa."

"You carry the king's seed. There is no other place for you than his harem." A gray-mantled eunuch grabbed hold of her arm.

"I will kill myself before I go to that fate," she cried.

Banu tugged on Esther's arm. "We should return inside." The three made their way back to the suite. Esther hesitated on the patio. "It is a reality to be faced."

Banu shook her head. "Everywhere you go, you earn favor from those around you. If anyone is to gain the recognition of the king, it will be you."

"A great if, indeed. What is life in the harem? Will it be as controlled as I am now?"

"There are more freedoms, but your life is not yours." Banu's eyes darkened. "Concubines who bear a child have more prestige than those who do not."

Esme sat on the wall surrounding the patio. "Solique says there are intrigues. Those considered wives vie for power and control of the children. Daughters can expect to be sent as slaves to the satraps. Sons who have more status can choose military careers."

"What of the women?"

Khepri joined them. "Now is not the time to focus on such things. Grace and merit are part of who you are. There is no need to worry you would fail in the harem."

***

Khepri spoke truth. Esther turned her thoughts to preparing for her visit with the king. Beyond that, what point was it to wonder and disturb her peace? Their days in Persepolis finally waned, and Esther's heart leapt at the sight of Apadana perched beside the mountains. Cleo jumped onto the bed as soon as Esther stepped into her room. She held her against her chest. "I missed you."

Cleo's purr suggested she had missed Esther as well.

Esme brought a tray with refreshment. Esther thanked her, then made a request. "Wait in the courtyard until you see Mordecai. He may still come every day and I long to hear news of him and of Susa. We have been gone four months."

Parisa swept into the room. "Three more months and you will be listed for your visit. We must refine your wardrobe."

Esther rolled her eyes. "I cannot possibly wear all I have now. What point is there in more clothing?"

"Styles have changed. What the king desires has changed. There is no fault in doing everything we may to insure you are well prepared."

Esther took a breath. "You speak truth. Let me rest before we start measurings and fittings." She let Cleo jump to the floor. "What I wish for now is a hot bath."

"I will have the servants heat water." Parisa glided away.

Esther shook her head as she glanced at Esme. "I do not think I will ever walk as gracefully as she."

Chapter: Preparing for the King

"Everyone is here." Esther observed the maidens who had become friends sitting in a semicircle in the main room. "Is something wrong?"

Jasmine stood. "All is well. We are here to celebrate. Your year of preparations is concluded. A date has been set for your visit with King Xerxes."

"When?" Esther felt her stomach twist.

"The first of Hanamakas." Jasmine took Esther by the hand and led her to a chair.

Esther's head swam as she translated the Persian month to her more familiar Jewish name. "Tivet? That is in a month."

Jasmine nodded. "You meet Hegai in a few days to make selections from the treasury."

"How do you feel?" Esme asked in Hebrew even though her use of Persian improved with practice.

"Scared. Excited." Esther named the emotions most easy to identify. But there was something else, something deeper. Determined was the best word to describe it, and yet, it was more. She had a sense of destiny.

Parisa stood and clapped her hands. "Treatments

may be over but there are plans to make. Zareen has one more Mehndi pattern to test. Banu must determine your hair and cosmetics. We need to select the gown and nightdress you will wear."

"I think simple is better than intricate. The pale blue dress."

Parisa frowned. "With the bare midriff? It is not a common style of Persia."

"I like the way I feel when I wear it."

Parisa tapped her chin. "We could add a fringe, a playful accent."

Esther nodded. "Something in silver like the scrolls in the fabric."

Parisa's smile showed she approved. She grabbed Esther's hands. "You will be perfect."

Zareen picked up a flute and played. As the whistling tune danced in the air, the other maidens formed a circle holding hands as they skipped and jumped. When a trill sounded, they stopped and clapped before grabbing hands once more and twirling in the other directions, skipping and jumping. After several minutes of the lively tune, they fell onto the nearest cushion or couch with a sigh.

Esme sat up. "We will come with you, into the palace, once you are queen?"

Esther closed her eyes. "If the choice is for me to make, you certainly will."

***

"Mistress Esther," Hegai bowed in greeting. "May the gods bless you always with grace and wisdom."

Days passed in a blur. Esther could hardly believe her turn to choose from the treasury of King Xerxes had arrived. She touched her forehead in response. "May you be honored."

He held her chin and studied her face. "You were beautiful when you arrived, now you are stunning."

Esther knew the light application of cosmetics enhanced her eyes. "You honor me with your compliment."

Hegai smiled. He placed a veil that covered her head and shoulders. "It is fitting that the king will be the first to see you." Though they met in the southwest corner of Apadana, he led her through the court to a wall with an image of a water fountain. He drew a leather strap from beneath his gray mantle and used the key to unlock a hidden doorway. The hallway went downward. Esther could not see what lay beyond. Hegai led her on.

When the hall turned to the right, Esther gasped. She'd had some image in her head of a few drawers of jewels, well picked over by this time. She thought wrong. Fire flickered in torches set throughout. Rooms filled with gowns reminded her of the colors of the bow in the sky. Tall cases overflowed with objects made from gold, silver, copper, and bronze.

Hegai stood at the entrance. "Find what you would like and place it on the table. I will have it delivered to your quarters."

Esther stared. "Choose what? How do I choose?"

"Is there nothing that pleases you?"

Esther opened her mouth but took a moment to respond. "This isn't about what pleases me. You know King Xerxes far better than I. What do you suggest?"

"It is not my place."

"Please." Esther looked from Hegai to the treasures and back. Then a thought occurred. "If something here were to please the king, he would have it in his rooms, not secreted away. I do not need anything, do I?"

"Come," Hegai said as he led her to a chamber of dresses. "You should not leave empty-handed. Queen Mother Atossa loved to wear jewels around her neck until she no longer could. Many of her favored pieces are stored here." He opened a cabinet. "Choose something of hers. Perhaps King Xerxes will remember it."

The selection was large, but not overwhelming. Each piece had been laid out as though the queen came periodically to look on them. Why could she no longer wear jewels around her neck? An intricate design with blue gems and diamonds set in silver that had been beaten into shape reminded her of the blue dress she'd chosen to wear. "I will take this."

"Nothing else?" At the shake of her head, Hegai smiled.

Esther felt as though she had chosen wisely.

Chapter: One Night with the King

Tebeth arrived, the tenth month. Trees across the garden boasted red leaves. Esther sat cross-legged in the house built for Cleo. She could see sunlight in the distance, but the shady spot for the house was cold. The short cape of black calfskin with fur helped keep her warm. Tomorrow would be bathing, cosmetics, hair, and Mehndi. Today was the quiet before the storm. She didn't know how to pray, nor exactly whom to pray to. So, she sat, in quiet contemplation, breathing in and out, listening for birds as Cleo purred in her lap.

Memory of those moments kept her calm as the preparations began the next day. No one said anything, though they all thought this could be the last time. Their last opportunity to help. Esme brought Esther's favorite foods. The main tray placed in the center of a table provided lamb, dates, hummus, and the red fruits Solique called tomato. Esther leaned against the tub with her hair encased in a treatment of coconut oil while Esme handed her pieces of meat. "I wish today were already over. That we would know our fate."

Khepri shook her head. "This is a great moment of many things. Wisdom is open to us."

Douika dipped a tomato in hummus. "The effort it took for you to learn to play the lyre speaks into your ability to play. Without the memory, the sound would not be as rich. We are all anxious for this day and your night with the king, but tomorrow will be all the richer for memory of preparing for it."

Jasmine laughed. "That is why I am not a teacher. I could not say such things as eloquently as Douika."

"I would not desire your responsibility for organizing all of this," Douika waved at the gathered group of women, "all of us."

Esther lifted her hands. "Each of you has been a blessing, far greater good than I deserve, but I am grateful for your friendship."

"You changed our lives, seems reasonable we should have some impact on yours." Khepri laughed gently.

Parisa clapped her hands. "Enough sentiment. We have work to do."

Their work proved worthy of great praise. After bathing, Esther sat for the haif ghalam arayesh, the seven items of cosmetics. Sefidab whitened her face, then Banu used ghazen to add soft color to her cheeks and zarak for a golden glitter. "What have you decided for the khal?"

Esther scrunched her nose. "Do I really need to have a beauty spot? The year of treatment did away with my spots."

Banu rolled her eyes. "No khal." She finished Esther's eyes with a copper tint that deepened the hazel color of her eyes. Banu waved at Zareen when she entered. "I still have to complete her hair."

Zareen looked at Esther. "Will you keep your hands still?"

Esther grinned. "As long as Banu doesn't pull my hair."

Banu laughed. "I am as gentle as a butterfly perched on a blossom."

Zareen pulled a stool to beside Esther's chair. A servant arranged a small table beside her. She started by painting the tips of Esther's fingers with the deeper color of henna, then drawing scrolls and vines with flowers down her fingers, ending in a circular medallion. She continued the pattern with a paler tint across the wrists to her lower arms.

All the while, Banu curled Esther's hair, parting the front since Esther would not allow bangs to be cut. She set a braided circlet of gold and silver with Kundan jewels dangling on her forehead. When Esther had finished preparations, her maidens stood around her. Esme and Jasmine blinked tears from their eyes. Parisa, Douika, and Khepri beamed. Zareen tilted her head. "You are stunning."

Jasmine nodded. "How do you feel?"

Esther removed the bangles on her wrists then traced the curling lines of the Mehndi tattoo. "Like this is a dream."

"It is time." Hegai arrived at the entrance to their suite.

***

"You are very beautiful." King Xerxes walked across the balcony.

Esther told herself to breathe. She'd seen his image, and the man standing before her held the regal air of royalty, yet he was a man of flesh and blood. A thin circlet of gold rested on his head. Thick curling brown hair touched his collar. The ballooning pants were a deeper blue than her dress, his shirt white, and a long red vest. She rubbed her arm. "Am I? Even a pretty face can darken with a bitter, cold heart."

He smiled, showing straight, white teeth. "Sumerian proverb. You have learning?"

She nodded. "I have been raised with a teacher. I speak different languages. I read and write."

Xerxes turned away. "What need has any woman for knowledge such as that?"

Esther laughed. "You can converse on more than weather and composition of fabrics. Why should I not as well?"

"What would you wish to converse about?"

She thought a moment. "The stars. When I was a child, we traveled from the mountains to Susa."

Xerxes turned from pacing, taking a seat near where Esther stood at the iron-twisted railing.

She continued. "The journey took many days. Every evening, father set camp in the direction of a star. The same star every night. We followed it here. You have traveled even further. Have you used stars to direct your way?"

"On darkest nights it seems as though milk spills across the sky. Sometimes stars are so bright you can hardly sleep for gazing at them."

Esther moved to a closer lounge and sat. "Most of our journey was during the moon phases."

"Stars are good for navigating, but not always reliable."

Esther grinned. "They battle with clouds."

"A battle indeed." Xerxes relaxed. "How many times did you make the journey into Susa?"

"Just once." She sighed. "There was a super harvest,

and my parents were taking grain to Egypt. They never returned. I stayed with the family who had taken me in."

"I am sorry. I am blessed to have my mother here."

"I have met her."

He frowned. "You met the queen mother?"

She nodded. "I can see where you get your strength."

"You think me strong?" His chest puffed.

"Not only in body, but in mind and spirit. You rule an empire. Even mistakes you make cannot break your control."

He stood. "Mistakes? Are you to tell me, Xerxes the Great, I have made mistakes?"

Esther squared her shoulders. "Would you rather I stroke your ego and say otherwise? Surely you gain wisdom through your experience."

He stilled. "Wisdom is not always easy to gain."

"But it is worth the effort? I am young. I have much wisdom to gain."

Xerxes returned to his chair. "You are young, but you are not unwise. What fuels your understanding?"

"I understand the pain of loss." Esther leaned forward. "Somehow, for me, that pain became compassion for others."

"Even here. I am sure you aided others in Shushan."

She shrugged. "Some, I suppose. It is an odd thing to be in competition with so many strangers."

"What do you think of the competition?"

"It is not what I envisioned in my youth, yet I cannot deny being in the center of Persia, with opportunity to see and hear and experience—I am not sorry."

"You are different." He crossed his arms and leaned back in the chair. "I have had women push me into bed before we have a meal. Others sit in a corner and cry for the night." He chuckled. "Some have loaded themselves with jewels to the point they cannot stand straight. That was my mother's idea, giving each of you access to the treasury." He studied her for a moment. "You have not done so." He moved across to her and pulled her to her feet. He touched the silver necklace she wore. "This is your only adornment?"

"I have a few more in my hair." His fingers brushing against her skin made her somewhat breathless.

"So, you do." Xerxes leaned down and kissed her.

Esther hadn't expected him to. Khepri had talked with her about the way of a man, but she said nothing about this intimate sort of touch that gently warmed her from the inside out. Some hours later, she woke with Xerxes the man sleeping beside her. He had been gentle, not like Khepri's warning. Esther felt her face flame. She had felt pleasure at his touch. She sat up and grabbed her tunic from the floor. Xerxes didn't move. She got up, ignoring protests of her body.

Torches provided light around the rooms. She crossed the floor in bare feet to look at a hanging on the wall. It was taller than her and seemed to be made of pictures. This first one told the story of a boy who fought bravely against an army. The sun and the storm sent aid and he was victorious.

She was examining the third hanging when warm arms wrapping around her waist made her gasp.

"Do you recognize anything?"

His nearness had her off kilter. She blinked and made herself breathe. "These are similar to carvings outside the temple in Susa."

"You will find them throughout Shushan as well.

They make renderings to be approved. I brought them here."

"Do you record your experience with each of us?"

"You will be the first."

"They have given their lives to you. Shouldn't each of them have a line of remembrance?"

"Their lives are already mine."

Esther turned and forced some space between them. "Yes, out in the world, our lives still belong to you, but life belongs to us as well. We had some freedom to make choices for our life. Here, we no longer get to choose."

"What if you were given freedom?" He touched her cheek. "Would you return to your home?"

His question stilled her. "This past year has been preparing me for something greater than anything I could imagine. I cannot return home."

She closed her eyes as he leaned down to kiss her. She didn't mind when he lifted her in his arms.

Daylight streamed through high windows when next she woke. Blood on the sheets spoke of what had happened in the night. Her hands shook as she dressed. Xerxes had gone. What did it mean? Would someone come get her and walk her to the harem?

***

Xerxes could not stop smiling, not even when Queen Mother Atossa invaded his rooms.

"You seem pleased." She sat in a chair near an opening that looked out on the city.

"I do not recall a meeting with you this day."

"What did you think of the girl?"

"I have been paraded with more girls than I care to remember. Why do you want to know?"

"This one is different. Of all the candidates I have

met, this is the only one I think capable of turning your head.”

“My head has not been turned.”

“Have you sent her on to the harem?” She asked, but from the gleam in her eye, he suspected she already knew that answer.

“She was sleeping.”

“My Lord,” Bigtha came into the room carrying a box.

Atossa jumped up. “I will leave you to your business.” Her smile widened as she exited his chambers.

Xerxes indicated Bigtha should put the box on the table. “Get Esther’s maidens and have them attend her. She may stay where she is.”

Bigtha said nothing, simply nodded that he would obey. He, too, had a large smile as he left the king’s chamber.

***

Esther stood as she heard noises. Something with which to brush her hair would be nice. As would food. To have her maidens enter stopped her fidgeting with her hair. “What is this?”

Khepri had no words, just wrapped her in a tight hug that made her tear up for some unknown reason. Khepri stepped back and took hold of Esther’s hands. “We are here to attend to your needs. A hot bath with oils will help.”

Esther spied Esme. “I am starving.”

Esme smiled, showing she understood the Persian words. “I will go at once.”

Jasmine stepped forward. “Parisa, get fresh clothes. Something for now, elegant for evening, and a nightgown. Zareen and Banu, you won’t be needed until later, but help Khepri prepare the bath. Master Bigtha, may you have water brought?"

Bigtha nodded and retreated from the suite.

***

Mordecai paced from the gate of the women's quarter to the kitchen garden and back again. Solique put her hands on her hips. "Stop with the useless journey. If you need to do something, weed the garden. The winter vegetables should not be neglected."

"Have you seen Esme? I must have news."

"I am here." The short woman hurried past Mordecai to speak to Solique. "My charge is hungry. Could you prepare a meal to send to the cardinal bedroom suite?"

Mordechai gasped. "She is still in the king's palace?"

Esme turned to him. "I came further than I needed because I knew you would be here. He has not sent her to the harem. He told her to stay."

Mordecai breathed out and sat on one of the benches nearby. "She has done it. She has won favor of the king."

"Do you think so?" Esme crouched in front of him. "Does this mean Esther will be queen?"

Mordecai shook his head. "We must not say anything until he has given her a crown."

Solique joined them, handing a basket to Esme. "Here are a few items. I will have a proper meal brought over when it is prepared."

"Thank you." Esme took the basket, said farewell to Mordecai, then returned to Esther.

Solique stood next to the bench. "You are pleased with this news?"

"My student has gained honor from the king. It

remains to be seen where that will lead.”

“I will take the meal and let you know if there is anything of import to report.”

Mordecai stood and grasped her hand in his. “Thank you.”

Solique blushed. “You can work in the garden while you wait for more news.”

He did not mind waiting to talk with her later.

***

With sweaty hands, Esther turned as a herald announced the king’s arrival. The day had been one of wonder, preparations almost as intense as the day prior. She pressed her hands against her yellow gown. Slaves opened the doors, walking backward. One placed a gold-covered narrow table against the wall. Another servant placed a plain wood box on top of it. Xerxes entered, and Esther’s attention turned to him. Long curly hair framed his face, held in place by a thick band of silver circling his head. High cheekbones and strong nose emphasized his position and power. The most powerful man in the known world walked into the room.

She moved closer, bowing low enough for her hair to swish on the floor. “May the blessing of gods be upon you this day.” She greeted.

“The gods are jealous of me this day.”

His grin brought a flush of color to her cheeks, but Esther did not quail. “Would you like refreshment? My cook artist prepared a platter of delicacies for you.”

He watched her for a moment, then nodded. Esther spoke to Bileg standing against a wall just inside the door. “Please assist in making my lord Xerxes comfortable. A carafe of wine is on the main table.”

He nodded. “I am honored by your request.”

His deep voice made Esther smile as she went to the other room for a tray. Fresh seafood had been delivered that morning.

Esme used a thin stick to arrange a shrimp more to her liking.

Esther shook her head. "You have outdone yourself."

"Solique provided while I assisted. I learn much from her."

"Thank you for what you have done." Esther took a deep breath as she lifted the tray. "You may return to our quarters." Esther did not comment on Esme's wide grin, nor her knowing look. She took the tray into the other room.

"What have we here?" Xerxes pushed up from his lounging position as she placed the tray on a round table between their chairs.

Esther tried to remember what she had been told. "The squid is sauteed with almonds in a light cream sauce." She knew that dish fairly well. "Clams and … and … the round things. They were baked into a cake." She placed her hand on her chest. "I do not remember the name."

"Scallops. The other is shrimp." He picked one up by its tail.

"Would you prefer Bileg request your cup bearer to attend you?"

He smiled but shook his head. "I am comfortable with you. Have you tried any of these yet?"

"Fish and crab have been the extent of my experience," she said with a shrug.

He handed her a shrimp. "Join me."

She took it, tapping her fingernail against the shell.

"This outer part is hard. Do you eat that as well?"

He laughed. "It is not recommended. Observe." He picked up a large shrimp. "Hold the back portion with your fingers and then pull the other end." He pulled and the shell slid away.

Esther copied his motions and cheered with success. "I did it!" She took a bite. "This is delicious."

"My mother visited with you." He smiled knowingly.

"Queen Mother Atossa? Not today, but yes, we have met. She mentioned you enjoy food from the sea. There were several of us in the room when she entered. She greeted everyone. Inquired when one of the girls sneezed."

"How did you get to speak with her?"

"Hegai introduced us. I am in awe. She has years of honor upon her, and yet she is the essence of a warrior, a mother, and a peacemaker. I do not know what else. So great a lady, and yet she conversed with me."

Xerxes ate the squid, and then gave her an odd look. "You have a way about you that puts people at their ease. You spoke with her in Prakrit."

"I appreciated the opportunity to practice."

"How did you learn so many languages?"

"My father was a merchant farmer. I would hear people speak words that made no sense to me. How people communicate fascinates me. My teacher took notice of my interest and provided learning opportunities. Once I learned symbols could be written to represent words on paper, he taught me that as well."

Xerxes leaned back, offering Esther the last of the shrimp. "You read these languages?"

Esther wiped her fingers on a cloth. "He taught me,

yes, though I've never had much access to writings to be truly proficient."

Bileg cleared away the tray. Xerxes snapped for his slave. "Take Bileg with you and bring me a scroll. Something from the histories, I think."

The men obeyed and Esther looked at him. "My Lord?"

"Please, my name is Xerxes."

Esther felt her cheeks heat at the honor he bestowed. "Xerxes." Saying his name please them both. "Do you mean to test me?"

He laughed. "If I desired a test, I would see how well you play the harp over there."

She smiled. "I have no experience with instruments. I dare say you would be displeased."

"I am to play the harp for you?"

Esther's eyes widened. "Surely, it is here as decoration."

He stood. "I have a little training."

His playful demeanor brought a laugh. She shook her head. "You do not have to play for me."

He took her hand and they moved closer to the instrument. "What if I want to?"

"Then I will be honored." Her heart quickened. He meant to do it.

Xerxes pulled the instrument further into the room, along with the stool beside it. He sat. His knees poked up. His outer coat swept back. He wore white linens that parted for each leg, allowing him to straddle the instrument which seemed larger than himself.

Though he did not have the skill of a true musician, he played a tune that brought to mind water flowing with a gentle touch over rocks. She closed her eyes to listen.

"Beautiful."

His eyes darkened. "You are beautiful as a summer wind on a clear morning."

Bileg and the servant returned with a scroll, and Xerxes stood. "That will be all. You may return to your evening posts."

Once they were alone, he handed her the scroll unopened. Esther unhooked the mechanism and rolled the scroll on the main table. Xerxes moved the decanter.

Esther ran her finger across the symbols the way she'd watched Mordechai read. "This is Aramaic." She lifted a brow. "Not very good with story." She circled a section with her finger. "This speaks of a farmer living outside the southern gate. He sought recompense for soldiers ruining the fourth field."

"What recompense was awarded him?"

Esther searched the section of the scroll. "No entries have been added to indicate he received compensation."

Xerxes stepped in to take a look. Esther gasped, then slapped his arm lightly. "You read as well as play a harp?"

He laughed, taking no offense at her touch. "Having a basic understanding of written communication is necessary for the king. Not all advisors are trustworthy."

"You are a great man. I pray you will always have good council close."

"Bileg offers good council. Let me get him and correct this error tonight." After going to the slave with orders, he returned to Esther. "What do you think is fair for the farmer?"

"And his family? My father grew grains. After harvest, he sold in the markets. In good years, he traveled to where the need was. Find out the manner of yield that was had that year. Pay him what he should have earned, or equivalent in supplies or herds."

He watched her with another of his strange looks. "You are a wise woman, even in your youth."

She tilted her head. "The farmer should have reasonable compensation. My idea would not have been hard to come by."

"Most other women I met would not care."

"That is their loss."

Someone entered. Xerxes took a step back. His stature increased and the closeness they shared dissipated. "Ah, Bileg. Did you bring your slate? I have a task for you."

The matter was addressed in a short time and an update added to the scroll. Bileg left with it to address the oversight.

"You act quickly."

"If I do not act on it now, something else will take it from memory." He crossed the room and picked up the box. He brought it to her. "Another swift act, but one I am certain is what I want."

Esther felt her heart stammer then speed up. The box lacked adornment, but Xerxes carried it as though it held great treasure. "My lord?"

He placed the box beside her. "You are not what I imagined, and yet you have captured my mind and my heart. None other has drawn my affection as swiftly."

Esther blinked. "I am honored by your words."

Xerxes removed the lid. Nestled on a nest of flower petals lay a circlet band. When he lifted it out, strings of diamonds and loops dangled. He placed it on her head. "A formal crown will be designed after the official proclamation. I have found the new queen of Persia."

124

Chapter: Bigsan and Seresh

"**The time has** come, my brother. Our flesh needs be avenged."

The larger man nodded. "His interest in his new queen distracts the king. That we are selected to stand guard at the doors is no small fate."

"I have waited years," his voice dripped with hatred. "To take from us such a light as my Vashti, may her beauty never diminish, and now none other province can command praise for he has chosen a woman of his own city."

"She is fair, fair, fair and garners much attention." He shifted position on the balcony and smoke drifted through the air around them. "Their death will bring about the change we need. What means do you have?"

The thin man smiled. "Among all the oils brought for the beauty processes of the virgins, has been valerian root. I kept the discards to use for a dire dosage."

"How will we manage to poison them?"

"We are the guards at their door, incumbent to perform whatever necessary duty they require through the night. There are none else. We are trusted implicitly. To us, it is, who must do this thing. You will stand while

I go to relieve myself. An evening platter of goods are delivered while I am gone, and they will have to leave it at the door until I return. It will be our pleasure to provide extra dressing to their meal."

"A fair plan, my friend. When will we do this?"

"Three nights hence, as the king's festival reaches its peak, there will be performance and story tellers in the wide hall. Much ale and wine will flow. The palace guard will be sent to monitor the masses. It is our most likely opportunity."

Mordecai recognized the tall, slender Bigsan, a eunuch of high regard. Never would he have imagined an assassination plot from him. His shorter confidant was Seresh. Him he could believe would make a plan. Three days? Not enough time to take the matter to the council for consideration. Mordecai did not want to believe what he heard. The fools spoke openly on a balcony, where they thought not about others who might be around.

"I dare not go to the King myself. I am too lowly to warrant such honor. Who else would listen to the likes of myself that could take this matter to the king?" His thoughts slipped to Esther. Her life was in danger as well. She would have to tell the king.

Reaching Esther had its challenges. He went to the kitchen porch. Warm wind blew in the morning light.

"Master Mordecai," The mistress of the kitchens blushed as she bowed greetings. "Shalom."

He nodded, touching his forehead. "You honor me. I wish to speak with Queen Esther. It is a most urgent matter."

"I am not permitted to go to her myself, but I can fetch her cook. You tell her what you need."

"I am grateful for your thoughts. Do you have time

to make the trek this morning?"

"I will. You may visit the garden. Esme will join you there."

Mordecai grinned. "What would you like me to collect while I wait?"

"Tomatoes and peppers are ripe. I think there may be figs as well."

He nodded. "Your basket will be full."

Esme proved a useful go-between, and Mordecai was permitted to enter the queen's garden. Unlike the dutiful kitchen garden, this garden was designed for pleasure. A symmetrical channel with fountains provided the noise of running water. Six quadrants, each blossoming with colorful flowers, drew him. Esther sat on a bench. She wore her crown, an intricate design of gold and silver set with red gems and sparkling diamonds. The crown was not as lovely as the light of her eyes when she saw him.

***

"Father Mordecai," Esther cried, rushing to take hold of his hands as they stood among trees of the orchard. "I looked for you at the gate during our procession yester-morning, but you were not there. My heart rejoices to see you are well."

"My beautiful daughter," he squeezed her hands. "Heaven bless you with the desires of your heart. I bring dire news for you."

Esther noticed the lines around his eyes. "What has you concerned?"

"Are you familiar with the eunuchs Bigsan and Seresh? I overheard their murderous plot, not two hours past." He relayed the details.

Esther's countenance darkened. "I will inform the

king and bring your name to his knowledge. Join me here tomorrow and I will share what transpires."

"Go with blessing," Mordecai kissed her hands.

***

She had to look at them as she entered the suite shared with Xerxes. Bigsan bowed his head, his face kind and respectful. Could Mordecai be confused?

Xerxes moved to welcome her. "Ah, my sweet. I hear we will enjoy delicacies of the sea with our meal this afternoon."

"I look forward to our time together. But first, if you will indulge me," she looked to the head of the guard standing close. "A terrible report has reached me, from your councilor Mordecai. Bigsan and Seresh who guard our doors through the night, have plotted murder."

Xerxes's hand tightened on the long pole attached to his throne. "Does this man offer worthy council, that I would turn on trusted guards?"

"He was my tutor all the years I lived in Susa. He often waits in the gate to hear news of me. This morning, he overheard two guards." She pressed her hand against her chest. "Our guards who watch over us through the night. He provided particulars."

His lips tightened. "What reason do guards have for murder? They are trusted men."

"It is a horrid claim." Esther lowered her face. "Yet, with your power and wisdom, truth may be sought. Make the unknown, known. They will not escape the diligent search of your Imperials."

Xerxes rubbed fingers against his beard, a sign Esther was learning meant he pondered to decide. He pressed lips to her temple. "As I said before, you are young but wise." With a nod to indicate his acceptance, he waved at the head guard. "You have heard the claim. Take your men. Search diligently and ascertain what is the truth in this matter."

The guard clicked and bowed, then went his way, taking three others with him. Xerxes motioned for the scribe to draw near. Xerxes offered his hand to Esther to pull her to her feet. "Tell him all you have heard." He turned to the scribe. "Record her account in the book of the Chronicles. Include the names of all involved. They shall each be dealt with as fits their works. Honor will be given where honor is due, and death to whom betrays the great king."

The man wrote.

***

"My Lord, the report provided by your councilor, Mordecai, has been confirmed."

Esther sat in a slender chair beside Xerxes. The men brought by the guards stumbled, tightening a leather strap around their necks. Their hands were bound in front of them.

"This is an affront, a travesty of misjudgment. Sar Rabu, great king, have I ever given cause to doubt my loyalty?" The taller eunuch shook his hands. "This is a misunderstanding. The liquid is a mixture I cultivate for tanning. It is a recipe given to me by an old slave last season we visited Persepolis."

"My lord," Esther leaned closer to the king and spoke in a quiet voice that still managed to travel. "I have a maiden in my employ, an Egyptian woman expert in oils. Allow her to check the liquid and determine if your servant speaks truth."

The king held her hand a moment. "You speak wisely, Queen Esther. We must ascertain if this substance is poison or something else."

Esther turned to her servant waiting nearby. "Have Khepri brought to us."

The prisoners were led to a side room as the court waited. Xerxes reclined closer to Esther, toying with a strand of her hair hanging loose. "I am sorry you must witness such circumstance on your visit to court."

"Do you hear grievances from all your subjects?"

"Thank the gods, that is why we have councilors and lower courts. Only those who are invited may enter this courtyard. To enter without permission is death."

"Unequivocally? Is there no means for mercy?"

Xerxes lifted his scepter. The body-length wand of gold and silver braid had a diamond fitted on the end. The diamond had been smoothed into a sphere, yet color and light flickered within. "This." Xerxes held it towards her, "is mercy. The person to whom I extend the scepter may approach without fear of punishment."

"You are a mighty man, my lord." Esther spoke with a touch of awe in her voice.

A gong sounded from the antechamber. The oversized doors opened and Khepri stepped into the courtyard. The royal blue walls heightened the darkness of her skin. Straight and tall, she walked toward the dais. Esther shifted in her seat, adopting the posture of the older woman. Khepri approached them until she reached the guards. She knelt, lowering her face to the ground.

Xerxes' nod permitted Esther to speak with her maiden. "We have a task I thought you could assist with. An urn has been discovered. We do not know what substance it contains. With your knowledge of oils, I thought you could identify the liquid for us."

Khepri stood. "I am honored to be of assistance,

Queen Esther." Esther wanted to tell her to forego the pomp and ceremony, but Khepri seemed to be enjoying herself. "If it is an oil substance from the warehouse, I should be able to identify it, whether it is pure or mixed."

Esther motioned to the table set beside a fire. "The liquid has been stored in the amphorae. Please, let us know what it contains. But be careful."

Khepri nodded. She walked to the table. The amphorae overlaid in gold had two handles. Because of its size, two servants dressed in silver cloth held the handles. Khepri lifted the ceramic stopper, then wrinkled her nose at the scent that wafted into the air. "This is not a good oil." She replaced the lid.

"You can tell that quickly?" Xerxes questioned.

Khepri knelt on the floor.

Esther held up her hand. "Be at ease, my lady. What do you think?"

Khepri stood. "The scent is not strong, but unmistakable. The warehouse used wormwood in the preparation materials. Thujone is a secondary substance. A touch can be added with wine and other alcohols for an effervescent experience, but much more can cause unpleasant effects."

"Could it kill?" Esther stared at Khepri, heart hurting. She didn't want to think someone would try to kill her.

"Yes, if enough were mixed with something that could mask the scent."

Xerxes flew to his feet. "Bring the miscreants." His shout shook the assembly.

"Come this way," Esther called for Khepri to stand behind her chair.

Xerxes strode to Bigsan and Seresh. He slammed

his scepter against the side of Bigsan's head. "I trusted you and provided you with honor."

Bigsan's face darkened. "Foolish and weak! You never should have returned from your failure in Greece. Vashti would be alive."

Xerxes grabbed the man by the throat. "Escort the queen and her maiden from this place." He spoke but did not release Bigsan. The slender man choked.

The guard ushered Esther and Khepri through a back entrance into the courtyard. Screams could be heard as they wove through hallways and into the open. Khepri wrapped her arm around Esther. The two of them shook. "I did not realize."

Esther took a shaky breath. "They intended to murder us, to poison us the day after tomorrow. Master Mordecai overheard them." They walked the length of Apadana, past the princes' apartments and around to the queen's garden.

The afternoon light made the trees gleam. The breeze blowing down the mountain was warm. Khepri breathed deeply. "We begin preparations to travel to Persepolis in a few weeks. Are the gardens as rich as these?"

"The land is greener. Gardens are more structured. Except for the woods. We were not permitted outside the women's quarters. I hope I can explore more as queen."

"We will keep you safe, my lady."

Esther smiled. "Thank you, Khepri. Master Mordecai will join me here in the morning. If you see Jasmine, would you send her my way?"

Khepri returned to their quarters while Esther walked along the path through the gardens. Thoughts of Bigsan and Seresh were difficult to banish. Why risk death? How could a man's heart hold that much hate? Esther prayed for them. For herself. For Xerxes.

LAURIE BOULDEN

Part 2
Chapter: Haman's Rise in Power

"That Jewish scum is why we continue in this place." Haman stood at the back door of his small house. The saving grace of the back garden was the palm tree whose branches swayed as a breeze blew across the land. Haman cared little for the view—walls and a pile of broken pottery piled against a neighbor's house. A cat jumped onto the wall separating him from the next building. He threw a stone at it, causing it to hiss before running away.

"You shouldn't do such things. You bring anger upon us from the gods."

"Attention of the gods is what I need."

"And such you may receive. Think no more on the little man. I have news that may interest you."

Haman frowned at his wife. "What news could you have?"

Zeresh rolled her eyes. "The market is a place of useful information if one knows where to listen and to whom to listen."

"You do?"

"I raise twelve children. There is much of which I

am capable. But, if you would rather not hear my news, I shall bother you no further." Zeresh turned to return to the house.

"Wait." Haman growled. "Speak your idea. I will let you know its value." He had sons to carry his future. Long it had been since he bothered with daughters or his wife.

Zeresh leaned against the open door. "A new bathhouse has opened near the temple. Soveign and Petre gather with their counselors. It is a common area where you could meet with them. Take advantage of opportunity to make yourself known."

He'd been prepared to scoff at her idea. Haman narrowed his eyes as he studied Zeresh. "Your thought is clever."

She nodded. "You are intended to be a great man."

***

Haman tied his towel around his waist as he entered the main room of the bathhouse. Rather than a series of pools for use, one large pool filled the space. Columns kept the low ceiling supported. Heat and humidity rolled through the air. A group of men already lounged in the pool. Haman placed his towel on a bench and stepped into the milky-colored water. Heat caused his feet to tingle. He walked the ramp, getting deeper, until water lapped at his waist. He settled a few feet from the others, far enough to be respectful, but fully capable of hearing and being drawn in if needed.

A large man with a shining crown of baldness and wreath of curling gray hair waved at Haman. "Did you see the hanging?"

"Of the servants who attempted a plot to kill our ruler?" Haman nodded.

Another of the men waved his arms. "Some think they should have been impaled. Left to rot on the hills."

"Having the birds peck at their bodies while they squirm on a stick?" Haman shrugged. "Would not have been too harsh an end for those who set themselves against the crown."

"I heard they intended to kill the new queen as well. That they had familial connection with Vashti." A younger man gossiped.

The older man hit him. "Get removed from my presence. Hers is a name not to be remembered or honored." He snapped at servants hovering nearby. "Take him from our presence. Remember and allow him entry no longer."

There was a brief silence as those assembled watched the young man retreat, head lowered. The large man turned to Haman once the disturbance ended. "Do you know who I am?"

"Master Soveign. Of course, I am aware of you."

"What is your name?"

"Haman, of the house of the Agagite."

Soveign tilted his head. "Agagite? I am unfamiliar."

"Many generations have passed since King Agog and his people were destroyed by the nation of Israel. My people are remnants that had been scattered at the time of slaughter."

"Israel? You mean the Jews? They are a scattered people themselves. One of many peoples residing in our fair Persia. To what do you aspire, Master Haman?"

"I studied many years under the tutelage of a priest, Xemea the Wise."

"Ah, then you are intended for work in the palace. It is a pity his untimely death affected your progress."

Another group of men wandered into the pool area, and several of the men with Soveign laughed and called for them to join. Soveign stood and walked closer to Haman. "Come to the gate this afternoon and ask for Thenwei. He will bring you to me."

Haman didn't mind the new men pulled attention from himself. Zeresh had been right. A good place to get noticed. Perhaps she had other ideas that could benefit him. He purposed to return attention to her.

***

"Haman, today is a good day." Soveign opened his arms.

Several weeks had passed since their initial meetings. Haman greeted the large man with traditional kisses to his cheeks. "I am intrigued by the message I received. How may I serve?"

Soveign motioned for Haman to walk to the balcony. "The council of Xerxes has lost one of its members. A carriage accident. Most of the council has aged. I think the king would appreciate a younger member."

Haman tried to conceal his ardor for the opportunity but the glint in his eyes gave him away.

Soveign smiled. "I thought you would be pleased. Take your time. Watch and listen. The king does not suffer fools unless he is in a merry disposition. If you wish to elevate yourself above others, give him cause to be pleased by your presence."

Haman considered his words as he followed a line of men into the king's courtyard. Like the Apadana, this space had walls of blue and gold. Intricate lattice work overhead provided shade from the sun. The carving of the beast with a lion's head was nearly as tall as himself.

Its teeth seemed to gleam as he walked past.

Along the wall on the east side were a row of tall-backed wooden chairs. They had been stained. Upon closer inspection, thin lines of paint etched into the curving strips of wood that made up the back of the seat added dimension. The backs were also tall, much taller than a man sitting down. A crescent mood had been carved at the top.

The king sat on his throne, one hand grasping the scepter and the other leaning on the arm of the chair. Thick curls fell below his shoulders. The head piece of blue stood out against the dark of his hair. This close, he seemed younger than Haman had thought. Thick lines of kohl outlined his eyes. His skin was smooth, unlike most others who battled against the dry air.

For the first few visitors, the councilors remained quiet observers. As the day progressed, two men entered, carrying a chest between them of red with gold overlay. Behind them walked a woman. She, too, dressed in red. Her hair had been painted gold along with her lips and fingernails. The men set the chest on the floor in front of the king. "Majesty and honor upon you." The woman spoke in a clear voice as the men moved out of the way. "I am Zgenshi, daughter of great honorable men of the To'chari."

"Welcome, daughter." Xerxes stood briefly and nodded. "What is your purpose in visiting?"

"We are a people of land. A great winter stole our leaders. I, alone, remain of the house of the kings. I offer you our treasure, treasure of the honorable men of the To'chari, that you may take in her people and protect them against the savage rulers who would do harm."

Haman studied the woman. It wasn't so much her

beauty, but her exotic nature that caught the attention of everyone in the room. An elderly man, seated nearest to the king, approached the throne. After a rickety bow, he leaned close. "There is room to add her to your harem, my Lord."

Xerxes stared. "She would be a lovely bird."

The woman frowned. "For a gilded cage? You mistake my purpose. I have not come to offer myself. Rich reward has been laden within the chest. I wish to return to my people with the knowledge of your protection surrounding our borders."

Xerxes' countenance darkened. "You refuse high honor within my palace?"

"My king, may I have council with you?" Haman jumped to his feet. What he knew of the To'chari was their craftsmanship and access to rare minerals and metals.

Xerxes narrowed his eyes. "Who are you?"

"Your grace, I am Haman the Agagite." He bowed low yet managed to keep his hat on his head. "Your councilor, Soveign, begs your indulgence in accepting me."

Xerxes straightened on his throne. "We shall see." He waved, indicating Haman could proceed.

Haman stood close and lowered his voice so none of the others could hear. "The To'chari live in a wild region, yet they carve life from the desert and pull treasure from mountains. You may be tempted by her beauty and exotic air. We all are, but you could do much better with access to the resources her people possess."

Xerxes held his gaze. Silence stood between them for a few moments, and then his face relaxed, his smile brought a light of friendship to his eyes. "Councilor, indeed, you are. You speak against my own words, and yet you speak wisdom. I am thankful for your presence here today." Xerxes stood and stepped toward Zgenshi. The woman stiffened but did not retreat. Xerxes stopped at the chest. "I will accept your offer. Let peace be between us, between the To'chari and Persia. In exchange for access to the resources your people have cultivated for some time now, I will order a battalion to accompany you home. Do you have accommodations for that number?"

"My uncle has an army, small in numbers and service. They may join forces, allowing your leaders to renew their purpose."

"It will be done." Xerxes pointed to Haman. "Bring Thenwei. Have him introduce Zgenshi to Queen Mother Atossa. Let her be welcomed."

Haman bowed and retreated from the courtyard. A gallery of mid-level eunuchs waited in the eastern room. Haman accomplished the task, and then returned to his seat against the wall. Deep breaths kept him from bursting with excitement. He'd been noticed by the king.

142

Chapter: Ailment of Queen Mother Atossa

"Mistress, you have a visitor from the palace." Jasmine interrupted Esther's lesson with a lute.

"Who?"

"She is a stranger to me, yet Thenwei is with her."

Esther handed her instrument to the slender elderly woman. "Thank you, we will resume in two days." Her eyes widened at the sight of the woman entering the chamber.

The woman bowed. "Forgive my intrusion. I have been told you engage an oils mistress who may know medicinal purposes for oils."

Esther nodded. "You heard true. How may we assist? What is the need?"

"I fear it is for someone you know far better than I. Atossa, the queen mother. She is ill."

Esther jumped to her feet. "I have not seen her in many weeks. What ails her?"

"There is a sickness in her flesh. She says she visited healers in past years, but her body grows weary and dull."

"Jasmine," Esther looked to her companion. "Find

Khepri and bring her to the palace, to the chambers of the queen." She turned to the stranger. "I am Esther, queen of Persia. I will go with you."

The woman bowed. "May the blessing of the gods be upon you. I am Zgenshi, a princess of To'chari."

Though Esther had seldom been invited to the elder queen's chambers, she knew their prominent location. Zgenshi spoke true. There was a putrid scent in the air upon entering. Esther motioned to Thenwei. "Open the windows, call for palm wavers." She hurried to where the queen sat in her gilded chair.

Queen Mother Atossa peered at Esther with furrowed brows. "Why have you come to disturb my rooms?" The queen was pale and gaunt. A wet stain seeped through her red gown on one side of her chest.

"I would have come sooner, had I known you were ill." Esther crouched beside her, grasping her hands. "Mother Atossa, you need not suffer alone. Allow us to tend you."

Queen Mother Atossa sighed. "I am weary. I would like to rest upon my bed."

"Let us tend your body. Look, here is Khepri." Esther smiled as Jasmine and Khepri entered the room.

Khepri motioned for Thenwei. "Prepare the bath chamber. The water should be warm, not hot. Send to the oil warehouse. We will need lavender, helichrysum, and frankincense first. Tell the workers to soak wraps in hyssop oil and bring them after an hour." She crossed the room and knelt before the queen mother. "My great lady, it is an honor privilege to tend you. Please accept my humble ministrations, that we may ease your comfort."

Esther felt joy at Khepri's use of Persian mixed with Egyptian.

Atossa nodded. "A bath would be lovely."

"Is your wardrobe specialist with you?"

Atossa shook her head. "She is gone by this time."

Jasmine jumped up. "I will fetch Parisa."

Once they had her soaking in the oiled bath, the queen mother's wound brought a bout of nausea Esther had been fighting recently. Jasmine led her to a candle of lavender burning near the window.

"This is an old wound," Khepri noted as she gently cleansed what she could.

"A bane that has returned after some time." Atossa rested her head against the copper tub.

"This poultice will help ease your pain, but it will not heal you." Khepri dried the queen's chest, then had servants bind the poultice of hyssop oil to the wound.

"I am not long for this world. The angels of my ancestors await in the windows and doors."

"Be that as it may," Parisa entered with a silken wrap laid over her arm, "we shall do what we can to ease your passing."

Atossa stood to allow Parisa to wrap her with the dark-colored wrap. "I await the Lord of Wisdom at the Chinvat Bridge." She sank onto her bed with a sigh. "I am ready for the scales of their judgement. Daena will lead me to paradise."

Esther sat beside Atossa on the bed, holding her hand. "How else may we attend your needs?"

Atossa smiled, patting Esther's hand. "Live your life long. May you also be mother of kings."

Esther kissed Atossa's forehead as the older woman closed her eyes to sleep.

***

As Queen Mother Atossa rested near an open

window, Jasmine and other maidens did what they could to clean the rooms and freshen the air by burning herbs and heating bowls of incense. When Esther returned to check on Atossa, the lemon citrus scent of the air was more agreeable. She strode to the older woman's side. Atossa leaned against pillows. Her long gray hair rested against her chest in a braid. She was still pale, but her greenish brown eyes seemed clearer.

Atossa reached for her hand. "Thank you for the aid of your maidens."

"Why have you not told us you were sick?"

Atossa chuckled. "I am old. To be old is to be sick."

"We are here to help you now."

"Angels have come to tend. There is no dishonor in that. I have been queen to two kings, and now my son rules." Her eyes drifted shut.

Esther studied the look of peace on Atossa's face. For all her years, few lines marred her skin. Her lips turned up in a soft smile, as though she had no fear of what was coming. Esther left her to sleep.

***

"My lord, Xerxes." Esther greeted the king as he entered the royal chamber they shared when he desired time with her.

He sat on the lounge and held his hand to her.

Esther smiled. "I am honored by your attention, but may I ask something of you?"

Xerxes frowned. "You have but to inquire."

"Your mother has taken ill. It would be best for you to visit."

He sat straighter. "Queen Mother Atossa? Why has no one informed me?"

Esther raised her brow. "You know the queen

mother better than I."

"She would do all she could to see I am not disrupted." He sighed, rubbing his eyes.

Esther placed her hand on his shoulder. "I will remain here, in case you desire company after your visit."

Xerxes took her hand and kissed it. "I will see you later."

Chapter: Death and Rise in Power

Death of Queen Mother Atossa halted daily practices within the palace and around Shushan. For three days, processions led by priests wandered through the old queen's chambers. Each day, provisions were collected in baskets and taken to the mound built in the mountains west of the palace. Esther watched from her window. Xerxes had come to her after visiting his mother. Then again, at her death, Esther bade him rest his head in her lap as she sang the few lullabies she remembered of her own mother. He slept and was gone when she rose in the morning.

Jasmine joined her on the balcony. "Parisa has acquired white gowns for the funeral procession. Khepri has the baths prepared. Zareen has been called. There will be time for Mehndi. Banu fears you will come to harm without protection."

"Banu has odd thoughts. How can designs on my skin keep bad spirits away?"

***

"Did the old queen die the way Aunt Talisha died?" Sammy's question pulled everyone from the story.

Sharine placed her hand on the precious book on her

lap and smiled at her grandson. "Many historians think Queen Atossa eventually died from breast cancer. Doda Talisha had cancer, yes, but a different kind. "

Sammy frowned. "Do we need to worry about evil spirits?"

She shook her head. "No, we do not. The One watching over us protects us from evil spirits."

"Are their funerals like ours, or did they put her in a pyramid?" Rachel sat up.

"Persian funerals were very different than ours. The mound where they buried her had an opening to allow the carrion birds to eat away her flesh until only the bones remained."

"Mother!" Camille stood in the doorway. "I think we should return to the story. Isn't Haman about to do something?"

"Oh, he is." Sharine studied the book in her lap. "Something very bad."

***

"I know you are enamored with your new queen, but there are ties to be strengthened with other territories. Marriage is the best way to secure our borders. It is time to visit some of the other virgins."

Xerxes felt as though a darkness lay on him. "Make the arrangements. Speak with Hegai."

Haman nodded. "A wise decision, Lord."

Xerxes stared at Haman. "The old vizier will soon walk the path the queen mother is walking. You will take his place."

Haman stilled, slightly blinded by the sudden onslaught of emotion. "Me, my king? There are other councilors who have served you far longer."

"That is of no consequence. I have spoken my

choice. Will you deny your king?"

Haman bowed. "Never, my lord. I serve you faithfully."

***

Soveign raised a glass to Haman. "Vizier. May your wisdom ever guide our majesty."

"I am honored. Service to the king has been my greatest desire."

"I knew when first we met, yours is what his majesty needed. Your youthful spirit will be good for him."

"I have more than youth to offer."

"I mean no disrespect, Haman. I am glad to see you raised to a higher position. What positions can you offer for our sons?"

"Our?" Haman stood. "I think you misunderstand. I do not intend to allow this relationship to influence my choices or actions."

Soveign's face darkened. "Never forget, you are here because I took notice of you. Where would you be without me? Don't imagine you can control this position without my assistance."

"Is that a threat against the high vizier of Persia? Do you think such threats go unnoticed?" Haman snapped his finger and a stream of soldiers marched into the room. "You heard him. There is a cold cell where he may repine. Be sure his family is banished to the province of Saka."

"Haman, why—" Soveign pulled against the soldiers holding him but could not break their grip.

Haman strode to within a breath's distance. "I am thankful for all you have done, but I cannot risk you would hold power over me." He spoke in a soft voice only Soveign could hear. Something in his chest twinged, but Haman refused to acknowledge any sentiment or regret. Zeresh was correct. To keep control of his new position would require that no one could lord it over him. He turned as Soveign was taken from the banquet.

A few days later, Haman entered into service as the Chief Advisor and High Minster of Persia.

Xerxes welcomed him to the great hall. "Ah, Haman, my friend. Have you settled into the royal house? I am sure where you were is a lovely place and your sons can manage it well, but as my newest high advisor, I thought it imperative for you to live close to the palace."

"Thank you, my Lord. I am honored. Mistress Zeresh is pleased with the view of the markets below the terraced gardens. That is all I need." Indeed, the new house was located in the royal section of Susa, where others of the king's family resided. They were still on the plateau, but instead of the wall, the side sloped down the valley. The gardens had been built to make the transition attractive from the view of those living above.

Xerxes offered his hand for Haman to kiss. After the act of fealty, he gathered his robes and returned to the throne. "Delegates arrive from a province beyond our borders. An agreement will expand our hold of Indian territory."

"How may I be of assistance with the transaction?"

"We require someone who fluently speaks their language. They will, of course, address us in Persian, but I do not trust their discrete discussions in their home language. I desire to know what is said."

Haman nodded. "The queen speaks many languages."

"These are the days of, Daena, Ashi, and Vata of the wind. Honor days for women mean ceremonies and secret rituals. I have promised not to disturb her. Find me someone else."

Haman bowed low, then removed himself from the main court of the king. He sauntered through the halls then out into the opening archways of the Apadana. He followed the road down to the Gate of Darius. As expected, the dual-sided building with open walls were not empty. Men of upper stations lounged on benches. Haman could hear them before he turned the corner. They quieted as he approached. Master Altier placed his fingers on his forehead and bowed his head. The others followed his example. Haman felt something within him stretch. He straightened, accepting their honor.

"May peace be upon you." Altier stood and offered Haman a seat of honor.

Haman arranged his robes and sat. Men present on the other side of the building moved closer, standing against posts and columns within listening distance.

"The splendor of King Xerxes' court brings subjects and visitors from distant regions of the empire. Their voices may not understand our language as we who have spoken it since our youth."

"You want a man who can speak other languages yet maintain native understanding?"

"You speak well." Haman nodded. "Whom would you recommend to his majesty?"

Three of the men conferred. Haman crossed his right leg over his left knee. "What is your thought?"

The man with a long, narrow face met Haman's glance. "Minister Soveign has vast knowledge regarding such things."

Haman kept his face neutral. "My esteemed mentor has been sent on a mission of great importance. It is beyond his power to assist in this matter. Do none of you have your own ideas?"

"My daughter had a tutor, a man from Susa. I've heard him in the market. He speaks with many of the foreigners."

"His name?"

He closed his eyes. "An unusual one, something… he is one of the Jewish immigrants. Mor… Mos…"

"Mordecai, of course." Another counselor slapped his thigh. "Excellent choice. Not only does he have a grasp of languages, but he is an honest man. His translation will be true."

The name made Haman's chest ache, but he controlled his reaction. "He is not an immigrant if he is of Jewish ancestors. He is a captured barbarian."

One of the men scoffed. "They have been among us far too long to be considered barbarians. Besides, if this is what is needed, are there other choices? Counselor Mordecai may be our only option."

Haman could not deny the logic, though he was loath to consider asking the man to attend the king's court. He swallowed his personal distaste for the need. "Very well, who among you can make the request? Have him at the north end of the Apadana by midafternoon upon the third strike of the sun." Haman glanced through the gathered men as he spoke, holding each with his gaze for a moment, weighing their worth. A smaller man with sallow skin marked with pots did not waver. Haman nodded. "I will meet you beside the Fountain of Ahura Mazda. The gods grant you success in your endeavor."

***

"The king seeks an interpreter, or rather, someone to listen and report." Nader grinned. "The new vizier demands your assistance, though he used flowers and shrubs to make his request."

"Me? How would I come to his attention?"

Nader laughed. "You are well known in the markets. How often do we come for your aid in our dealings with foreigners? Of course, you are well known." Nader sat on a stool beside Mordecai. "You will be too practical for a royal court. If they don't appreciate you, much harm could come of it."

"There are some who will be pleased to see me." Mordecai held up his hand when Nader opened his mouth. "Say nothing. I have charged her to remain silent with it, and so must you."

"It is not like you to recommend deceit."

"I have charged none to give false witness. My heart warns there is purpose to this. I do not understand how, but I believe."

"That is all I require."

***

Nader's visit changed Mordecai's plans for the afternoon. After the sun passed overhead, he walked along the canal road and then up to the gate. Afternoon sun hid behind clouds easing his journey. An unusually large group of men loitered between the twin buildings of the gate. Mordecai chuckled to himself. The vizier's visit caused quite the stir.

Nader stepped forward to greet him. "Shalom."

"Shalom Aleichem." Mordecai responded. Some of the others appeared uncomfortable with their Jewish greetings. Mordecai turned to a familiar mentor, Master Altier. "Blessings to you this day." He resorted to the common tongue.

"Mordecai," Altier said as he pressed close to Mordecai's cheek. "Have you seen the king's selection of the new vizier?"

Mordecai shook his head. "I have not. I suppose it is Soveign, or one of his circle."

"Soveign is nowhere to be found." Altier frowned. "He has departed on an important mission no one knows about."

"Then whom?"

"Haman, the Agagite, son of Hammendatha."

Mordecai grinned. "The young man who's offer of assistance was refused? Is he aware I am that man? He does not seem like one who would forgive."

"Perhaps he has matured. Or he is wise enough to realize he needs you for this, whether he has forgiven the slight or not."

***

From the hard glint in Haman's eyes, the man had not forgiven, nor had he forgotten. Mordecai continued walking toward the fountain.

Haman had thickened in the past few years. He had also hardened. A muscle in his jaw twitched, yet he said nothing to Mordecai. Haman pulled his cream coat with purple ribbon together as he turned. The guards beside him indicated for Nader and Mordecai to follow.

A slender eunuch in traditional robes with purple mantle greeted Mordecai. "The supreme Vizier welcomes you in the name of Ahura Mazda and directs your attention to his special purpose. Prince Jie of India and his entourage will greet our royal majesty Xerxes on the morrow. You are charged with listening to their conversations and reporting to his grandness the vizier."

Mordecai lifted his brow. "Listen to private conversations? How does that fit our purpose?"

Haman frowned. "It is not your place to determine value in what has been spoken, merely to obey."

Mordecai intended to question Haman's wisdom, but Nader kicked his leg and Mordecai remembered Haman no longer held a low position and causing trouble for himself would not prove wise. He lowered his head in a traditional sign of meekness. He didn't need to feel it in his heart, merely show it on his face and by his actions.

***

A large party arrived by caravan, moving through the city with some difficulty as people of Susa ran to ogle the strangers. Mounted soldiers wore striped pants of gold and gray and bare chests protected with leather armor. Turbans were wrapped around pointed metal hats. Behind the horses rode several carts pulled by matching oxen draped in richly colored blankets. Most carts were filled with men, the first being Prince Jie and his advisors. Women filled the third cart. They were all dark haired, with large buns held in place by colorful sticks. Their dresses were like robes wrapped around them and tied in place with wide ribbons beneath their breasts. The colors were shades of blues and reds.

Haman led the procession to greet them. Royal soldiers dressed in yellow uniforms and holding long bows spread to either side of the Gate of Darius. Haman bowed to Prince Jie, bending at the waist. Prince Jie jumped from the wagon. He rolled his arms and bent nearly to the ground.

Haman greeted the visitors, directed Prince Jie to select two of his guard to accompany the group to the great hall, then led them slowly through the grandeur of the Persian royal court. The room to the north of the main entrance had tones of green, from the soft fern print on couches and lounges, hunter green fabric paper on the walls, and chartreuse pattern in the flooring. The blues and reds of the women's dresses stood out. Mordecai moved to the side. He'd been directed to wear dark green robes, and since he was accounted as a servant, none paid him heed. There were nine women in the party, all dressed in the same wrapped gown. Its height above the ankle marked them as high servants, and yet, two of the women seemed to receive pampering and attention beyond any of the others. Why would the emperor disguise two of his daughters?

Ceremonial and customary interactions took nearly an hour before Haman called for the dignitaries to be taken to a waiting suite where the prince would be refreshed. Xerxes sat upon a small throne between two long windows. "I am unsure what he hopes to accomplish with gifting us a dozen female slaves."

Haman stood near the king. "We have placements for his gifts."

"If I may," Mordecai stepped closer and lowered his head.

"Who is this?" Xerxes asked.

"The interpreter. Did you hear something?"

"A strange thing, indeed. You say the prince spoke of the women as servants, yet his daughters are mingled with them."

"Daughters? How can you be sure?" Haman scoffed.

Xerxes frowned. "Why would he treat his offspring such?"

"If he were to force you to wed them, it would not be to your advantage."

"Yet, if I refuse his gift, I set enmity between us." Xerxes looked at Haman. "What are we to do?"

After a few moments of silence, Mordecai offered a solution. "It is not an uncommon practice to brand slaves."

Haman nodded. "If they were to go through the branding, the daughters could never claim a station above that of servant." Haman slid a glance at Mordecai. "This is one way to be sure they know their place."

Xerxes smiled at Haman. "I see the wisdom in your idea. We will know by their responses how true an offer has been made."

Hours later, Mordecai watched the procession pass beyond Shushan, its women protected. The deck also overlooked the gardens near the kitchen, but he noticed no one working.

"Master Mordecai," Esther called as she walked out of the palace.

Mordecai welcomed her with the traditional kiss on the cheeks. "You are radiant, my daughter." No one was around to hear his endearment.

"The celebration of Daena and Ashi brought refreshing."

Mordecai's face darkened. "I know you are caught in a foreign court, but never forget to whom you belong."

Esther lowered her gaze. "I take time with Esme to worship, but you speak true. To be drawn into the pagan world comes too easily."

"I will offer sacrifice for you. Be strong, my daughter."

"Esme shares that you assist Solique."

Mordecai smiled softly. "The gardens for the kitchen grow many blessings. I am pleased to be of good help."

"Esme learns many things from her. They create dishes for special occasions. I wish we could have you join us for dinner. If our relationship were to come to light…"

Mordecai shook his head. "Now is not a good time. Have you met Xerxes' new chief advisor? Haman the Agagite of the house of Agog. He carries a grudge against the line of Israel."

"You think there is risk to me?"

"He is not to be trusted. Best your heritage remains hidden a while longer."

"How do you know Minister Haman?"

Mordecai chuckled. "He requested to assist me when there was no need. He did not take refusal well. It is through Soveign he has risen to power." Mordecai rubbed his beard. "Yet, Soveign disappeared shortly after the new appointment."

"There is no reason for you to cross paths now."

"The king's court required use of a language master. Haman did not appreciate having to use me, but there is none other in Susa."

"The king's court?" Esther faced Mordecai. "You have not mentioned this honor."

Mordecai shrugged. "Having to eavesdrop does not feel like an important role, though I was able to prevent an entrapment of the king."

"I am thankful to hear your tidings. I grow fond of my husband."

Chapter: A Challenge to Bow

"Walk with me." Xerxes moved Haman to the center of the procession. Where the king wore royal colors of blue and green in his silk robe, Haman's new robe wove soft peach and deep red in long stripes. Soldiers led the procession and followed behind. Other courtiers and councilors remained a few steps behind. Haman watched those beyond the procession. Heralders captured attention of citizens. Everyone stopped what they were doing. People bowed, some standing, some groveling on their knees. Haman's heart swelled.

Xerxes noticed Haman's pleasure. "An experience to savor."

Haman laughed. "These are the people for whom I strive by your side. I feel as though I can perform amazing feats."

"Your position reaches even above those of the princes of Persia. Why should you not have privilege and standing in support of your work?"

"What are you saying?" Haman noticed they neared their destination temple.

"Let it be known," Xerxes raised his voice and a scribe scurried to his side. "Let it be known, High Vizier Haman the Agagite, highest minister to his royal majesty, Xerxes the Great, shall receive benefit and honor due his great station and his connection to one as holy as I. Consider this commandment, servants of myself, those within the royal house of Shushan, within the city of Susa, and those without, shall surely bow down before Haman. Reverence to him is to give reverence to me."

Haman had to press his hands against his side to keep from reacting to the joy brought about through such a declaration. "Your majesty, what have I done for you to honor me thus?"

Xerxes laughed. "Meekness is not a friendly coat for you to wear, your grace."

***

Haman held his head high as he entered Susa through the main gates. Counselors, eunuchs, and servants bowed. Mordecai frowned. To the king he could choose to bow in acknowledgement of his position. Haman was not a king. There was no reason to bow.

"Have you not heard the decree?" A counselor stepped closer to Mordecai after Haman had cleared the gate. "We are to bow down to the new Prime Minister. The king declares it."

"Minister Haman desires worship. I am a Jew. I cannot bow to him."

"I do not think you can call on your ancestors as a reason not to obey a king's command."

"I am one man. What notice would he give me?"

Mordecai gave the matter no more thought. He went to the market.

***

"Husband." Zeresh reached for Haman when he stepped onto the balcony. Birds chattered in a tree as he sat beside her on a bench. She blossomed in his renewed interest. Her dark hair glistened. A pale stain heightened the color of her lips. "The seasons will turn toward summer. Will we remain in Shushan when the king's house retreats to Persepolis?"

"Do you think the king will go without his Prime Minister?"

"I have never been. Now we will visit as royalty. All honor and glory shall be afforded us." Haman frowned, and Zeresh raised a brow. "You do not think so?"

"There is one who does not give me respect that is due."

"Who would refuse to obey a command of the king?"

"His name is Mordecai. He is a captive from Israel. Claims he is a Jew. He cannot obey, for to do so is to displease his god."

"The only god he need fear is the one who sits upon the throne. How do you know of his dissent?"

"Counselors have reported his insolence."

"Do not allow him to continue. If other Jews see there are no repercussions to disobeying the king, they will follow his example."

"The nation is a nuisance." He thought silently for a moment. What would it take to rid him of Mordecai? To rid Persia of the Jews. Not to allow them to return to their home. Oh no, that would make them an asset to enemies of Persia. Was there a way to destroy them completely?

Zeresh squeezed his hand. "You have won wealth and prestige. Use it to your advantage."

Haman considered his options. "The festival of Shanti begins. There are things we can accomplish with the power of the vine."

164

Chapter: A Note of Joy

Esther leaned back from the foulness in the bowl and closed her eyes as Jasmine wiped her face. "Thank you, my friend." Esther sighed.

"I have not seen you ill before."

"This is not an illness." Esther grinned, though her insides clenched.

Jasmine's eyes widened. "How would you know?"

"Khepri thought it so. I must send word to the king."

"So soon? You do not show."

"If this is a son," Esther pressed her hand against her belly, "he will usurp Vashti's son. Until there was a possible heir, he had no reason not to keep Darius in the palace."

Jasmine gasped. "I never considered. As high queen, your son will be next in line to the throne."

"It has taken years. I thought perhaps I was to remain barren."

"Why would you think that?"

"Punishment for getting too close to the gods of Persia."

"Then this is indeed good news. Your god has opened your womb."

Once the nausea passed, Esther felt restless indoors. She crossed the room to where Jasmine drew on parchment. "Our year has nearly ended. Lavender should be in bloom. Let us go to the gardens. Where is Esme?"

Jasmine motioned to the dining pavilion. "Chinese couriers brought you a gift of lace and fabric. I think it is pure silk, a gift worthy of royalty. She will have it hung along the walls."

"We should go see."

The fabric was truly amazing. The pavilion had two walls of screens. Silver loops were screwed into wood. The fabric hung like curtains. It was a rich green on which images of flowers and birds had been painted. Esther touched the fine material. "Great talent went into making this."

A long, low table sat in the center of the pavilion. A thicker white material with the same images of flowers and birds swept over the table. Cushions of deep burgundy were round about the table. A taller buffet set against one wall. Dishes, silver, glassware, spread across the buffet with a vase of flowers in the middle. Esme rubbed a silver goblet with a soft cloth.

"This looks fit for a banquet." Esther praised as she turned to take it all in.

"Mistress Esther," Esme dropped her towel and greeted Esther and Jasmine.

"I could invite the king and a few others." Esther lifted a finger bowl.

"Oh, not yet my lady." Esme glanced around, panicked. "I will get it prepared. I promise, I will let you know. A month, not much more."

"Very well. I wanted to go to the gardens to pick lavender. Are you able to join us?"

"Oh, yes. I want to ask Solique what flowers she will grow. Spring and the new year will be upon us soon."

Chapter: A Note of Sorrow

He should be happy. Haman studied the obeisance of a group of slaves as he passed. But in the background stood Mordecai. Xerxes gave no notice, but for Haman, every moment seemed to speak disrespect, a stiff neck. The feast of Mazda arrived. King Xerxes celebrated with the princes and high peoples of Persia. Haman lounged beside the king, enjoying the sway of palms offering a cooling breeze. Haman raised his glass. "My king, highest among the gods. All honor and glory is due you."

Xerxes drank, then held his cup to be refilled. "It is good to be worshipped."

"But not by all." Haman crossed his feet. "There are a certain people scattered and dispersed among the provinces of your kingdom. They do not keep the king's law, nor do they worship the king."

Xerxes face darkened. "Within my precious Persia? Is this to be born?"

"If it please the king," Haman continued, "let it be decreed they be destroyed. I will pay into the treasury ten thousand talents. There can be no concern that the king's business will suffer loss."

Xerxes toyed with the signet ring on his third finger.

Haman pushed. "Allow me to do this for you. Set to right your subjects."

Xerxes enjoyed more of his drink. "You know best how to use money to my benefit. Keep it that you might prosper us both. Do with the people as seems good to you." He pulled the ring from his finger and handed it to Haman. "See to the matter yourself."

Haman took the ring. The hammered gold shank seemed surprisingly plain. The seal was a garnet bezel incorporating a star and crescent moon.

"Put it on," Xerxes waved his goblet. "You do not want to lose it."

Haman enjoyed the rest of the festivities, but he eagerly awaited the opportunity to put his plan into place. Days later, after the feast had been celebrated, he called for scribes and priests. "Cast the pur," he demanded of them. The collection of bones rattled in stone cups used by the priests. They poured their lots on the floor. Haman peered at the first set. Twelve. The month of Miyakannas. Too long, as far as he was concerned. He went to the next casting. It, too, was twelve.

"The gods have spoken, Lord." The eldest priest gathered his bones into his cup, shook them for a moment, then poured them out again. "It will be the day of water, the thirteenth day." He nodded, "a fitting day it is. Water to wash clean."

"What do you want the decree to say?" A scribe set papyrus in a screen.

Haman walked to the windows. "This decree is to go to every prince, governor, and official of all people in all provinces of Persia. It is written in the name of King Xerxes." Haman lifted his hand to reveal the seal. "It will be sealed with the king's own signet ring." He took a breath, then stared at the scribe. "Write. On the thirteenth day of the twelfth month, you are bidden to destroy, to kill, and to annihilate all Jews, young and old. Women and children included. All of them, in that one day. Those who do so may plunder ill-gotten goods of the dead. Make yourselves ready unto that day." He looked to the scribes. "Locate that dog, Mordecai, he who refuses to bow his head in reverence of his betters. Find him and have him make the necessary translations."

***

"Minister Haman calls for you," a servant addressed Mordecai as he sat on the front porch of his home.

"I would not think he was up at this hour."

"He has been working since before light touched the sky."

"Must be important." Mordecai stood. "I will go with you."

Though they walked through the quiet morning, Mordecai could elicit nothing from the servant. The man refused to meet his eyes. He was brought to a room in the Eastern court. A series of tables had been set up. Scribes worked on parchments.

"This way, master." The servant led him to the first table. "You are to write in the language of each province as you are able."

Mordecai pulled a written form toward himself to read. His blood turned cold, and the pit of his stomach became as stone. "This is a joke." He stared at the nearest scribe.

The man shook his head, tears in his eyes.

"I cannot write this," Mordecai's hand shook.

The scribe moved closer. "You want them to have no warning? Do you wish to hide what is coming from them all?"

Mordecai closed his eyes. The scribe showed wisdom. Jews everywhere needed to know. Somehow, some way, salvation would come. He knew not how or from where. Tears wet the parchment as he wrote.

The walk home afterwards passed in a blur. Mordecai knew not if he passed a friend or if any other spoke to him. The sun shone overhead, yet he felt as though clouds covered all. Gray mists were all he could see. Once he reached the front porch of his house, he could go no further. He fell to his knees, a wail of anguish piercing the air. He tore at his shirt, as though ripping away the Persian civility could somehow ease the pain.

Nader ran to his side. "What has happened? Where are you hurt?"

Tears soaked his beard and he struggled to speak. Words would not come. He covered his eyes and wept. Time passed. He drew a shaky breath. Nader remained, face gray as though he knew something horrid had befallen them.

Mordecai gulped. "The king has broken faith with us. He has charged through all the provinces that the Jews are to be destroyed. Put to death as though our lives have no purpose or meaning." He glanced at the torn fabric across his chest. He grasped it with his hands and ripped it away.

"What are you doing?" Nader tried to stop him, but Mordecai went into the house.

"Is this to be born? Am I to wear the clothes of those who come to destroy us? Are we to bow without regard to our own lives?" He took hold of a long sack laid against the kitchen wall, dumping its contents on the floor. He took a knife and ripped an opening for his head.

"You mean to wear that?" Nader questioned.

Mordecai added holes for his arms. The sack fit over his head and fell against his knees. He rubbed his hand in a bin of stove ashes and swiped it across his head and face.

Nadar stepped to Mordecai. "What madness has overcome you? There must be mistake in what you say."

"There is no mistake. I had to write many copies in many languages for provinces across Persia."

Nader paled, causing the marks on his face to stand out. "But how? Why? Why would the king consider such an action?"

"It is his minister, Haman the Agagite." Mordecai paced through the house. "I thought his hatred was for me, yet he has set the nation of Israel at peril."

"To what end? What does he accomplish?"

"Beyond ridding the world of us? I know not. Jews are in all areas of government and commerce. The loss…"

"The loss will be staggering. He has not thought it through. He has not considered the consequences. Surely, he will not go through with the plan."

"The proclamations already contain the seal of the king. There is no undoing. The law precludes all other actions."

Nader choked. "What of Hadassah? Will the king kill another queen? Who would dare raise a sword against her?"

"She is protected for now. She has not revealed herself." The thought did not bring comfort.

News of the impending doom spread like fire through Shushan. Voices rose in distress. Shining sunlight could not seem to break through the gloom. Quiet voices murmured through the market.

***

"I must go to Hadassah. I must speak with her." Mordecai finally roused himself.

Nader rubbed tears from his face. "Is it wise to make a connection between yourself and the queen? Should we not keep her safe?"

Mordecai sighed. "If we are to die, how safe can she be? Will her maidens be protected as well? There is no hope for us."

Nader had no reason to keep Mordecai from going. The tone of the streets was disturbed. Cries could be heard. Strangers pondered the meaning of the decree. He could hear them through the open windows of the ale house. Mordecai followed his usual route, but before he could step into the gate house, a short, thick-shouldered soldier lowered his spear to block the way.

"You may not enter the place of the king so dressed."

"I am a minister of Persia."

"Matters not. The king forbids the wearing of ashes and sack cloth."

"Then here I will wait." Mordecai slid to the ground outside the gate. Wails pierced the afternoon.

***

"My lady," Esme called, rushing into Esther's lounging room.

"What is it?" Esther jumped to her feet, noting the paler of her friend.

"Mordecai sits in the gates."

Esther frowned. "Of course, he does. He converses with visitors and elders from town."

"No, my lady. Not this time. He has dressed himself in cloths used to store tubers and roots. Ash stains his face and hands."

"Sackcloth and ashes?" Esther dropped into her chair. "But why? What has happened?"

"I do not know. They keep him from entering."

Esther went to her desk and pulled parchment and a writing utensil. She placed them in a bag. "Take this to him. Tell him he must write and inform me of his distress. I am high queen of Persia. Why should he suffer?"

Esme took the bag. "I will wait for him to write and return with his answer."

"Thank you," Esther said as she grasped her hand for a moment. "Go with grace."

Esther paced, though she knew it would take time for Esme to get to the gate. Time for Mordecai to write what ill had befallen. At the death of her parent's they'd grieved, wearing ashes. There were no other close family ties.

She moved to the south-facing balcony. She could see part of the market. It was a warm, spring day. There should be activity. Even noise like a faint rumble, but things seemed quiet. She closed her eyes and still she waited.

When the squeak of the door sounded, Esther ran across the apartment.

Esme handed her the letter. "It is a strange day in the city. Guards said I am not safe. What has happened?"

"Does Mordecai still wear sackcloth?" At Esme's nod, Esther gave her a folded robe and pants for Mordecai. "Ask him to dress and come to me."

"I will try." Esme accepted the clothes.

But the letter from Mordecai was ill-written. Esther sought Jasmine. "Send me Hatach. I need him to speak with Mordecai."

A few minutes later, a tall black man bowed. "My queen, how may I serve you this day?"

"Mordecai sits outside the gates dressed in sackcloth and ashes. He refuses to dress that we may speak within the palace. I must know what has befallen him. Why he has turned sorrowful."

Hatach bowed again. "I will speak for you. Await me here, my queen."

Esther did not like to wait. She moved restlessly from room to room. On the balcony overlooking Susa, she could hear mourners. The city itself seemed distressed.

It was nearly an hour later when Hatach returned. His face had a tight, grim look that caused Esther to fear. Her hand touched her belly as if to protect her unborn child. "What is it?"

"My queen, such tidings have never crossed my lips. The whole city is perplexed. The grand vizier, Haman the Agagite, has decreed with the king's ring of power that all Jews within Persia are to be destroyed. They are to be killed, to the child."

Esther's heart went cold. "How can that be? Why would Xerxes permit such a thing?

"Haman promised ten thousand talents to the treasury."

"Where could he gain that sum? I cannot believe it."

Hatach held a wrapped parchment to her. "Haman caused Mordecai to write these himself in the languages of each province. Swift horsemen and heralders have been sent to inform the provinces. Already, you can hear cries of the condemned."

Esther took the parchment but did not open it. She crushed it against her chest. "What are we to do?"

"Mordecai declares you are the solution. You must go to the king, make supplication unto him and make request for your people."

Esther stood. "I cannot go into the inner court without summons. Anyone entering without being called, the law is to put them to death, unless the king holds the golden scepter to them. That is the only way they may live." Her unborn child, she couldn't risk him, could she? "I have not been called to the king for thirty days. It would be foolish to do as he requests. Let me ask him to find a different way."

Hatach left with a bow, but his face remained grim when he returned. "His reply is not what you want to hear."

Esther stood near the balcony where color from the setting sun lit a background of red and gold behind her. "Tell me."

"Do not think yourself that in the king's palace you will escape any more than all the other Jews. If you keep silent at this time, relief and deliverance will rise for the Jews from another place, but you and your father's house will perish. Who knows whether you have not come to the kingdom for such a time as this?" Hatach offered the words faithfully.

Esther closed her eyes. "For such a time as this?" She was high queen of Persia. Above all other women, she had been shown preference and honor and prestige. Could there have been a purpose? She drew in a breath. Somehow, the scent of lavender from the freshly cut flowers in the next room wafted to her. It was the scent of peace and determination. She knew what she would do. She looked at Hatach. "Tell Father Mordecai to gather all the Jews of Susa and hold a fast on my behalf. Do not eat or drink for three days, night or day. I and my maidens will also fast. On the third day, I will go to the king, though it is against the law. If I perish, I perish."

Hatach bowed. "I will remain with Mordecai. Peace be upon you, my queen."

Esther blinked tears from her eyes.

Esme waited in the next room, face ashen. "What is to happen to us?"

"Only time will tell. Call the others."

Chapter: A Plan to Risk Death for Life

Esther waited until all seven of her maidens were seated in the room with her. Khepri smiled, unknowing of what had transpired. "I fear your secret has already been made known, my dear."

Esther's eyes darkened. "My secret?"

"You are with child."

"That is not why I have called you." Esther stood and walked to the mantle. "For six years I have not revealed a truth to you, though I suspect, some have guessed." She looked at Esme before continuing. "Mordecai is not only my tutor. He is, by blood, my cousin. When my parents died when I was young, he became my father. I am a Jew, a child of the people of Israel."

Douika gasped. "The decree."

"Yes." Esther sobbed. "My people are to be killed for what purpose? To what gain? It makes no sense, but that does not change what has been sealed with the king's ring."

Khepri stood. "We get you to Egypt. You will be safe there."

Douika nodded. "Or to my people beyond the

sunrise. You will not be harmed."

"My dear friends," Esther closed her eyes, overcome with love for her maidens. "You are precious to me. I would have you take Esme and Solique, but that will not save others from this horrid matter here in Persia. What manner of queen would I be if I were to run and hide rather than fight for my people?"

Zareen shook her head. "But what can we do?"

"I have determined to go to the king. In three days, I will enter the inner court without his invitation."

"But that is death," Zareen protested.

Banu jumped to her feet. "We will not permit such a thing."

"Father Mordecai gave me a thought that I must consider. What if I have been brought to this position in this place for such a time as this? I may be the only one who can save the Jews from this tragedy. I do not know how I can bring about salvation, but I am asking you to fast and pray with me for the next three days. In three days, on the day of Arshtat justice, I will go to the king. If I perish, I pray you will take Esme and Solique to safety. But may it be we find a way to save all my people."

Bright moonlight did not brighten Esther's countenance through the evening. Esther lounged near the balcony where she could see fires burning in Susa. She closed her eyes, wondering where Mordecai and the others would gather. Her heart poured prayers long into the night. There was little sleep. The young one within seemed to cry with her. When morning came, and nausea wracked her body, she could do little more than dry heave. She pressed her forehead to the cool tile floor and prayed for her Jewish brothers and sisters. Her friends.

Their families. For all the little ones about to be born and for the elders who waited on an angel to carry them to paradise. She prayed for Esme and Solique, for all they were and would be. She prayed for her unborn child, that he would be more than his father and the men of Persia who permitted such heinous deeds to be considered and decreed.

By the third night, her head swam, and she found it difficult to do much more than lay watching the setting sun. Prayer for herself and the others were not so many words, and yet, something poured from her heart. How quickly night passed. Esther could barely breath as she stood in front of the oversized doors leading into the inner courtyard of the king. Cold blew through the hallway with a sickening smell. Esther pushed against the door. A groan drew attention of all gathered around the king's throne. Their faces turned from smiles to darkened frowns. Xerxes' eyes bore into her. He said nothing, simply staring as she hesitated. But then she stepped into the room. He raised his arms, pointing at soldiers.

She tried to hurry. If she could reach him, he would soften his cold gaze. Soldiers captured her before she could touch the dais and reach for the golden scepter. Someone grabbed hold of her hair, pulling her head up. She could see her eyes reflected in the smooth metal blade of a sword. Fear stared at her. The blade moved.

Her scream woke her, jerking her up in the bed, heart pounding and face wet with tears. Clammy darkness surrounded her. She drew a shaky breath. Was death that close? She moved to the balcony. Night rested over them. Stars, distant and cold, sparkled in the sky. She drew a breath. The giant angel constellation, Kesil, raced overhead.

"He is a sign for spring," her father had told her, holding her hand as they gazed across the night sky.

"Is spring a good thing?" Hadassah stared, imagining seeds falling to the earth.

"Spring is hope. It is the time of new life."

"Hope." Esther repeated the word her father used. Hope is what she needed. She remained on the balcony, sometimes dozing, sometimes praying and watching the angel lead its minstrels across the night sky.

Morning came. Parisa and Khepri entered her chamber.

"My lady," Parisa bowed. "We have prepared a bath with rose oil and a steaming of lavender."

"Rose?" Esther sat up. "Such a rare oil."

"This is a special day."

She tried to focus on the ministrations of bathing and dressing. Banu and Zareen joined them. Banu designed Esther's hair in a complicated twist with dark flowers. Zareen covered Esther's hands and feet in swirls and khalkubi symbols of protection.

Zareen dipped a paintbrush in a bottle. "I harvested the leaves early so this mixture will dry quickly, though it will not last long. I will redraw later with a richer batch."

Esme entered the chamber with a tray in her hands. "I do not bring sustenance, but some burning of oils and herbs to set us all at peace." She placed the tray on a cabinet against the wall. She used a flint, and then a tiny flame burned. The sweet smell of sage drifted through the air. Rose, lavender, amaranth, and yarrow blended for an uplifting aroma. The women paused in their work, breathing deeply.

Jasmine smiled. "Smells like hope."

"Have you prepared a feast for our plan?"

"Yes, my lady, all is prepared. Solique and I have been fruitful with our fasting."

"Let us finish this." Esther held her hands above a basin so Zareen could rinse the henna paste from her skin. Banu finished her cosmetics with a khal drawn beside her lip. Esther studied the beauty spot in a reflective surface.

Parisa wrapped Esther in her royal robes using the wide belt beneath her breasts to accent her figure. The deep blue made her eyes rich and glittering. Once sandals were wrapped around her feet, Esther stood ready. Parisa grasped her hands. "May the gods watch over you and protect you."

Esther breathed. "There is but one I need concern myself with. Shalom." She looked at her gathered friends. "Wait for me here?"

Their nods and watery smiles made Esther's eyes sting. She blinked. There was nothing more to say. She would return to them. Or she would not.

Stepping from her suite, Esther felt alone. Hatach or any of the other eunuchs who usually went with her had been sent away. He would have stopped her or gone to Hegai to stop her. She walked into the garden, heading to the gate leading to a path she could take around to Apadana. The fountain gurgled but the colors she passed seemed dulled. The sun hadn't risen enough to reach the mountains to the west, and she walked in shadows. The buzz of a bee swirled through the air to her left. Birds called from a nearby tree. The normal sounds did not calm her mind or still the shaking of her body. She met no one as she walked the path and turned onto the ramp leading up to Apadana. Sunlight stretched across her slender feet wrapped in sandals. She couldn't feel the warmth, though she clenched clammy hands. Then she passed between the towering columns.

Something in her stomach turned. The sound of her shoes scuffing on the marble as she walked the length of the Apadana seemed like loud groans. *Go back. Hide who you are. You are not meant for this. What does it matter if the rest of them die?* She closed her eyes, fighting the urge to slow. Move one foot in front of the other. Step by step, drawing closer to her destination. Drawing closer to her destiny.

The gardens she could see beyond the building bloomed with spring colors, yellow and magenta and purple and blue. Sunlight made the colors rich. Someday, her children would play in the garden, hiding behind tall stalks, giggling as she searched them out. Children who would need to know their heritage. Her back straightened. Preserving the lives of her people did matter. She placed her hand on her belly. The one growing within needed to know Mordecai. Needed to hear the stories of the one who brought them out of Egypt and established their place in Canaan. It might not be home to the Jews at this time, but someday.

She turned into the inner corridor. She reached the eastern court. The long room was empty, as was the courtyard. She sidestepped a puddle and continued into the palace. On one side were the personal quarters of Xerxes. It wasn't the rooms they shared, but she knew well enough what lay beyond. She closed her eyes and took a breath.

She could hear talking. She could hear birds chattering. The time for flight was past. She turned to the inner court. There were no doors to open, she could see across the space. And be seen.

Xerxes sat upon his throne on the far side of the inner courtyard. He wore the wide cylinder crown with crenellated decoration. A thin veneer of deep blue covered gold metal. On one side, the jeweled image of a bull kicking the air reminded Esther of the reliefs carved along stone staircases throughout the palace. Her heart skipped as she caught his gaze. A hush fell on those in the room, but it was on Xerxes that Esther kept her attention. The moment seemed as long as life itself, yet his eyes lit, and he stood. His smile made the emptiness within her fill. She stepped into the room.

There were no jeers, no rush of soldiers to drag her to the ground and to her death. The king stepped down from the dais. The scepter clacked on marble once, then he held it toward her. She approached and touched the tip of the scepter. Weakness assailed her limbs, though she strove not to show it. Xerxes took her hand. "You are pale, come." He led her toward the throne and motioned for a chair to be set beside him. "You are welcome, my queen."

Esther sat, fighting an urge to collapse on the floor. "Thank you, my lord. I am overwhelmed by your generosity."

He returned to the throne. "What is your request, Queen Esther? It shall be given you, even to the half of my kingdom." He shifted the scepter to his other hand and reached for her.

Esther grasped his hand. "So great a place, it is beyond me to put my request into words. If it pleases the king, my maidens have prepared a pavilion and I would invite you and your greatest advisor to attend a feast in your honor. Minister Haman, isn't it?"

Xerxes smiled. "He is indeed one who has risen in power and stature, for the glory of Persia."

"Please," Esther smiled as her courage rose. "I invite you and Haman to a feast I have prepared."

"A feast with the queen is an unexpected pleasure." Xerxes waved for one of his eunuchs. "Bring Haman quickly. He is attested great honor this day and I am eager to hear him accept."

Chapter: Plotting Death

Bows of servants and guards barely registered as Haman stepped through the gate. An invitation from the queen? A rare privilege since she did not cater to parties or gatherings, as befitting her youth. But even with his head held high, he did not miss Mordecai. No obeisance from him. Not even a nod or a gaze turned away. Mordecai held his stare until Haman passed. *The glory and honor of position matters naught if this man... this Jew continues to humiliate me.* By the time he reached his home, he fell dejected onto a sofa.

Zeresh noticed his dark mood. "What ills has today brought you?"

Haman sighed. "I have been invited to eat with the queen tonight."

Zeresh sat across from him. "With the queen? Is that not good?"

"It should be, but how? That pig, Mordecai, sits in squalor in the Gate of Darius."

Zeresh grabbed his hand. "Are you not the second most important man of Persia? What is this man to you but a law breaker? What happens to those who break the law?"

Haman fisted his hands. "They should be put to death." He stood. "Call the servants. Have them fetch our friends. Let us seek council together."

Within the hour, the front rooms of Haman the Agagite's house were filled with people of Shushan, those he trusted to suit his purpose. He paced across the tiled floor. "Have I not been given wealth and riches? Blessed with ten sons?" He placed his hand on the shoulder of his eldest, Parshandatha. "The king himself promoted me above all, so none is higher than himself as I. Our young queen invites only me to come with the king to the feast she prepares." He paused a moment to hold the gaze of each of them gathered. "Yet all this is worth nothing to me, so long as I see Mordecai the Jew sitting at the king's gate."

Zeresh wrapped her arm around him and leaned against his side. "He is an evil in Persia, not to be born. There is no law that says you cannot have him put to death."

Others nodded. "And such a death, none other will dare to dishonor you, my father." Aridatha stood beside his brother, Parshandatha.

Parshandatha grinned. "What of gallows? Built to stand above all else in Shushan? In Susa itself? There will be no end to the honor that is due you and your offspring."

Zeresh nodded. "Build the gallows fifty cubits high, and in the morning, go unto King Xerxes and make known the need to hang Mordecai."

Haman swallowed his shout of glee, but nothing could hide the gleam of intent from his eye. "Yes, you have brought an excellent notion to me. Call for the workers. They are at my bidding. Use the strongest wood and the freshest rope to prepare the gallows." He kissed Zeresh' cheek. "I have a feast to prepare for."

Before he left the house overlooking the gardens and market of Shushan, Haman heard the workers preparing the gallows. The sight of Mordecai in his sackcloth and ashes, staring with righteous indignation, did nothing to upset his return to the palace. By morning, the man's cloth would be waving in a wind as life was strangled from him. He grinned. It was almost more than he could hope for.

Hatach bowed, greeting Haman as he entered the palace grounds. "High Minister Haman, the King requests you accompany me to his rooms. You will go together to Queen Esther's feast."

Though Haman could only stand in the doorway, what he could see of Xerxes' private rooms revealed opulence he had not imagined. Wood floors gleamed. Dark walls shimmered with fillets of gold and silver. The light that hung in a corner seemed to be of a thousand crystals amid bowls of burning oil.

"Bow, you fool," Hatach struck his arm and muttered.

Haman remembered his duty and bent as the king joined him. The doors closed. He considered making his request of the king now, but the gallows wouldn't be prepared, and he didn't want anything to risk an evening with the queen. Xerxes was in no mood to converse, so they walked in silence.

Hatach led them to the pavilion at the fourth hour after noon. Esther sat on one of the cushions at the table. Xerxes went to her. "Greetings, my lady. You look lovely this afternoon." He stopped her from getting up but took the cushion at the table beside her.

Haman bent at his waist. "Your invitation is an honor and a pleasure. I am astonied to have been invited."

Esther smiled. "I hear much of the one who has risen in power and what you have accomplished because of it." A bell announced the arrival of the first course. "Ah, a feast of delights awaits you."

Veiled servants filled goblets with wine then set a bowl of oregano, mince, and garlic doused with olive oil amidst a platter of flat bread. Esther took a piece of the herbed bread before motioning for Xerxes and Haman to have some.

"Your pavilion is perfectly situated, my dear. One may forget the long days of summer draw near."

"Persepolis is more pleasant. Will we visit the ocean again?"

"Haman will work in my stead. My presence will not always be needed."

"No? Isn't your seal required in many instances?"

Haman lifted his hand. "The king's signet ring. We are of one mind. It is my honored duty to serve in his capacity."

"Indeed?" Esther said nothing further as servants brought a new course. Broiled lamb in stew pleased the men, but days of fasting left her without wanting any. She nibbled the flat bread as the others ate heartily.

"These hangings are exquisite." Haman touched one of the green curtains after he finished. "Whose talent forged them?"

"Dignitaries from China," Esther answered, then glanced at Xerxes. "Is that right?"

"It is," he agreed. "Your use adds to its value. I do not think I have enjoyed a feast as wonderful as this."

"Your pleasure is all I require." Another servant filled the wine.

Xerxes raised his glass and grinned at her. "Yet, I think there may be something else? What is your petition? I will grant it. Your request to half the kingdom shall be fulfilled."

Esther breathed. "My lord, I have been exceeding blessed by your company this day, and that of your companion, Haman. My wish and my request, if I have found favor in your sight, if it please the king to grant my wish and fulfill my request, let the king and Haman come to the feast that I will prepare for them. Tomorrow I will do as the king has said."

A light in Xerxes' eyes brightened, and Esther knew he looked forward to their time together.

Chapter: Plotting Reward

Restlessness tugged Xerxes from the comfort of his bed. He wanted Queen Esther, but knowing she was with child, her first and quite young herself, he did not want to risk the life of their offspring. He walked the length of his room, through the outer chamber, across the balcony, and still felt no inclination to return to his bed. The young men guarding the door of his suite opened at his beckoning.

"Bring the book of memorable deeds. Tell the scribe to choose one of the chronicles to read to me. I wish to know valor and honor."

He returned to the balcony, staring at stars as he waited for the scribes. He heard the pedestal being set in place and returned to the outer chamber. Xerxes lounged on the sofa. One of the servants arranged his robes to cover his bare feet.

"My lord," the scribe bowed," I am prepared to read."

Xerxes waved for him to do so.

"Mordecai, a lesser counselor, told how Bigtha and Seresh, two eunuchs who guarded the threshold, sought to lay hands on King Xerxes."

Xerxes sat up. "What honor or distinction has been bestowed on Mordecai for this?"

The scribe searched the record but found nothing. The young men also shrugged. "Nothing has been done for him."

"Who is in the court?"

***

Haman could not sleep. Returning to his house, he could see the gallows standing complete against the darkening sky. Even as night approached, the deep wood stood out, blocking stars. Pleasure filled him at the sight. How soon could Mordecai be brought? Rope tied about his neck? He would be sure they knew not to tie it too tight. He wanted to see Mordecai splutter and kick against the slow encroachment of his throat, to see gasps as he tried to get air into his body. Anticipation made him tremble. He considered going into Zeresh, to share with her what would soon be. Moonlight crossed the pillow, her face peaceful if not given to beauty. He changed his mind.

"I will go to the palace, await the king," he muttered to himself. "As soon as he awakens and agrees with my decision, I shall pull Mordecai from his slumber. Breakfast may not yet grace the table before he hangs high above us all." He took a lantern to guide his way in the dark.

He entered the empty courtyard. Flickering torches lit the space. He thought to lie on a bench until the king stirred in the morning, but guards at the king's private quarters waved him over.

They bowed to him. "The king seeks council. It is a sign of the gods you are here." The man on the right opened a door and called inside. "Haman is here standing in the court."

Haman heard a joyous shout. "Let him come in."

Haman entered at the king's bequest. The king remained lounging on the sofa. "What is to be done to the man whom the king delights to honor?"

Haman blinked. Honor? *Whom would the king delight to honor more than me*? He considered what privilege would best be bestowed upon himself. "For the man whom the king delights to honor, let royal robes be brought, which the king has worn, and the horse that the king has ridden, and on whose head a royal crown is set. And let the robes and horse be handed over to one of the king's most noble officials. Let them dress the man whom the king delights to honor and let them lead him on the horse through the city. Let the proclamation be made as the people of Susa take note. 'Thus shall it be done to the man whom the king delights to honor'." The king's smile of approval left Haman feeling giddy. What more could a day possibly hold? He listened eagerly to hear his name, to hear the orders.

Xerxes clapped. "Hurry, take the robes and the horse, as you have said. Forget not the crown and the high honor of yourself as herald. Do so to Mordecai the Jew who sits in counsel with my wise men. Leave nothing out that you have mentioned."

Haman started in disbelief. He had misheard. Having Mordecai on his mind tricked his ears. He was about to open his mouth to confirm when the scribe lifted a writing tool. "I will write the honor given to Mordecai the Jew. All the world will know what great deed he has done, and what great reward has been given."

Haman held back the choking sob and dread. He stepped from the chamber of the king and gave orders to the eunuchs. "Bring me robes of the king, something he has worn. And the yellow crown with red rubies. Meet me at the stables. I will have the king's stallion brought out."

The men exchanged glances. "While it is dark?"

Haman noticed the open roof of the outer courtyard remained dark. He sighed. "At first light. The city will know the honor of Mordecai as they rise from their beds."

Haman didn't bother going home. He waited at the stables.

***

Mordecai rubbed his eyes, then realized the pounding was at the door, not in his head. News of Hadassah? He jumped from his bed. Instead of one of her servants or maidens, it was a pair of guards in the king's livery. His heart skipped, but then he noticed a white horse draped in the king's blanket. Had she told the king of their connection?

Bigtha stepped forward. He bowed, then offered the clothes on his arm to Mordecai.

Mordecai frowned. "What is this?"

"High Minister Haman the Agagite has the great honor of escorting you through Susa as the king's delight."

Mordecai frowned. "I cannot wear these. I am in mourning."

Bigtha raised a brow. "Refuse the honor of the king? This is in reparation for your actions that saved his life. It has been recorded in the book of the Chronicles. There is no refusing."

Mordecai looked past Bigtha to Haman. The man stood with a stoic expression, holding the horse. Honor a man to whom he declared death? Something beyond understanding was working. What had happened with Hadassah? What had brought this about? Rather than question further, Mordecai accepted the clothes. "Let me wash and I will be back."

He used a cold tub of water to wash away any signs of ashes before donning the king's clothing. Never had he felt the smooth touch of fabric nor worn such true color of yellow and blue. His shoes seemed inadequate as he sat on a bench on the front porch.

"Here, use these." Bigtha handed him a pair of silken slippers.

The time came to approach Haman. The man bent at the waist. "Counselor Mordecai, his majesty, king of Persia, declares you are to be honored this day. Please, take your seat on the horse."

Mordecai expected the horse to shift or suddenly jar him from its back, but it did not.

Haman held the rein. "Bigtha, the crown."

Mordecai filled with wonder as he took the golden crown from the servant and placed it on his head. Royal, indeed. He felt as though death itself could be conquered.

Haman stepped into the street, leading the horse. As they moved along the road, he began to shout. "Thus shall it be done to the man whom the king delights to honor." Over and over, he repeated. Turning, leading, guiding them up toward the palace, across Shushan, down into the marketplace, through the gardens, and back into the dwelling places of the people of Susa. Hours later, though the sun had not reached its zenith, they returned to Mordecai's house.

"I will bring the clothes as soon as I am changed." Mordecai said as he jumped from the horse.

"Do not bother. They are yours to keep."

"I am moved by the king's generosity."

Haman handed the rein of the horse to Bigtha. "Return the steed to his stable." With no further word to Mordecai, Haman departed. Mordecai stood in front of the house, watching the younger man. As he reached the corner, Haman pulled a hood low over his head. Mordecai's lips twitched.

***

"Are they coming? Did they bring him?" Zeresh ran past Haman to the street. No one followed. She turned back to Haman. "Surely he did not refuse you?"

"Refuse me?" Haman pulled the hood from his head. "Have you not heard the disturbance this morning? I walked the length and breadth of Susa heralding the wonder and honor of Mordecai the Jew for saving the life of the king." His face paled. "There will be no hanging today."

Others joined them as the morning progressed. "Where is he?" Parshandatha demanded as he entered the house.

"Hush," Aridai caught him too late. "Father is not in a mood. He has had to honor the Jew, not declare his death."

Parshandatha glared at another of his younger brothers. "Do not jest."

Aridai explained the events of the morning as another friend approached Haman and Zeresh. "There will be another chance."

Zeresh shook her head. "To think so is folly." She faced her husband. "If Mordecai, before whom you have begun to fall, is of the Jewish people, you will not overcome him but will surely fall before him."

"You mustn't say such things." Haman pulled away from her.

"Minister Haman," someone called from the front of the house. "Honored guest of the queen, she awaits your attendance to her feast."

Haman could never have imagined wanting to decline an invitation from royalty, but he was sorely tempted. Something warned him, his lot was about to change.

Chapter: A Plea for Life

Esme and Solique produced a second meal of excellence. Hummus flavored with olives and pine nuts was served on rosemary biscuits. Skewers with beef, tomato, and chicken braised in a spice bath were set in golden bowls. Esther offered a plate of honey cookies after servants cleared the other courses.

"Your maiden arranged this portico to perfectly capture the breeze coming down the mountain." Xerxes praised again.

"I have been blessed in all my maidens."

"May you continue to be blessed." Xerxes took her hand. "What would you ask of me? It is yours, up to half the kingdom."

Esther fell to her knees and took hold of Xerxes' hand with both of hers. "If I have found favor in your sight, O king, and if it please the king, let my life be granted me for my wish, and my people for my request. We have been sold, I and my people, to be destroyed, to be killed, and to be annihilated." A sob caught on her breath, but she continued. "If we had been sold merely as slaves, men and women, I would have been silent, for our affliction is not to be compared with the loss to the king."

Xerxes rose to his feet. "Of what people are you?" He still held Esther's hand.

"I am a Jew, of the house of Israel. Not a month past, a decree with the king's signet has been sent to all provinces in Persia." She stared at Haman. "We have been betrayed, accounted for slaughter."

"The Jews? But they are masters in matters both civil and economic. Who would do such a thing?" His roar stirred the fabric covering the walls.

"A foe and an enemy, this wicked Haman," Esther's voice dripped with accusation and sorrow.

Horror struck him at the betrayal of his friend. Xerxes clenched his fists. Without a word he strode from the pavilion. Esther staggered to the white couch set against the green fabric covering the wall. Her heart thundered in her chest and she closed her eyes to collect herself.

Haman's sudden presence beside her caused Esther to cry out.

"My lady, I did not know." He tried to grab her hand. "Please tell the king to spare my life."

She pushed him away with a gasp. "What are you doing? Leave me be."

"Will you assault my queen in my presence in my own house?" Xerxes shouted.

Haman fell back. "My king—"

Two soldiers pulled Haman from Esther and covered his face with a hood. Esther leaned against the back of the couch, her hand against her chest. Xerxes moved to her side.

Harbona stepped forward. "My king, this very day, Minister Haman intended to kill Mordecai, the man whose words saved the king. He built gallows fifty cubits high at his house."

Xerxes didn't bother looking at Haman. "Hang him on it." The soldier had turned when Xerxes cried out, "wait."

Esther heard Haman snivel. "I knew you would not do this—"

A soldier hit Haman, stopping his speech.

"Hold out his hand," Xerxes ordered.

The soldier gripped Haman's wrist and yanked it toward the king. Xerxes removed the signet ring, gripping it in his fist. With a wave he indicated they should fulfill the sentence of death.

***

Zeresh stared at the column of soldiers and people of Shushan marched up the hill toward her house. At first, a great joy overwhelmed her. Mordecai the Jew was to be killed, even with the high honor afforded him that morning. But as the crowd drew near, joy faded, and fear entered her. The man caught up between the soldiers was no stranger. It was Haman. She ran into the street. "What has happened? What are you doing?" She tried to reach Haman, to pull him free of the soldiers.

Someone pushed her away. "He is condemned. He plotted to murder the innocent."

"Innocent?" She screeched. "There are no innocents among the Jews."

A soldier grabbed her by her jacket and shoved her out of the way. She fell in the dirt. "This is king's business. Get in our way and you will hang with your husband."

She gasped. "You cannot mean to do this."

Haman remained silent as they took him along the

path beside the house to the gallows. They didn't remove the hood but wrapped one end of new rope around his neck and secured it with a knot. Other men pulled on the long length of the other end. Three pulls set the rope tight. A soldier arranged the knot at the base of the back of Haman's head. "Pull." He shouted.

Haman gurgled as his feet lifted off the ground. His body jerked. He reached for the knot, but there was no way to disengage. The sound of bones breaking could be heard as they lifted him further still. Soldiers sprang back as wet dripped from him. They didn't bother raising him the full fifty cubits but secured the rope so his body would swing until they received orders to remove him.

Zeresh ran to her house. Haman had built the gallows so they could observe from the balcony. She stood, gripping the banister, watching as they pulled him up. She could tell when his body stopped twitching. He was dead. She dropped to the ground and cried.

Soldiers found her there as they returned.

"What are you doing in here?" She sobbed as they surrounded her.

"This is not your place. Be gone."

She stood, her face pale. "Of course, this is my house. These are my things."

"Not any longer."

***

Xerxes held Esther as the soldiers took Haman from them. "I do not understand how this could happen. I trusted him. When he spoke of a people, I thought he meant our enemies."

"I told you my parents died when I was a child. I did not tell you about Mordecai, my father's nephew. He raised me. By his guidance, I kept my people and kindred secret."

"Mordecai? The counselor who saved my life? Who saved us?"

"The same." Esther smiled.

"You have family? You need more space than the suite of rooms we have in the palace. Take the house that belonged to Haman. We will have it decorated to please you. It is the best, save my palace of course. Mordecai can join you." He looked at Esther's belly. "Our child can grow there."

"Are you sure?" Rearing a child usually took place in the haram.

"Of course. Take your maidens with you. It will be a place I can meet with you outside the palace. We will send for crafters. They will prepare it for you while we are in Persepolis." Xerxes looked around. Harbona remained nearby. He waved to his attendant. "Send for Mordecai. He is to attend us in the throne room."

When Mordecai arrived, Esther rose to greet him. With the family relation noted, there was no reason to stay distant. She hugged him.

Mordecai had tears in his eyes as he gazed upon her. "You look well."

"I am well. Come, the king has news for you."

Mordecai bowed. "My lord, how may I serve you?"

"I hear you are a trusted advisor. Not only from your cousin." Haman removed the signet from his finger. "I chose poorly in my previous high minister. May you serve Persia with wisdom." He handed the ring to Mordecai.

He stared. "I am a lower counselor. There are others who would be better for this."

Xerxes smiled. "And yet, I have made a choice." He

smiled at Esther. "Show your house to your cousin. Let him know what you will need. We already know Mordecai can handle building projects."

"Your house?" Mordecai asked as they left the throne room.

"He has given me the house of Haman. I suppose there will be servants and such. Should we get rid of them all?"

"Without knowledge of them? You need to hire an overseer. One of the eunuch class who will be your businessman."

"Hatach is my most trusted eunuch. I will set you in charge, then the two of you can take care of matters."

"For a little while, at least. There is still the issue of the decree to destroy all of us."

"The decree? Haman is dead. What does it matter now?"

"It needs to be undone. News must be sent to each of the provinces. There is to be no battle against the Jews. Without that notice, all our lives are still at risk."

Esther pressed her hand against her head. "I did not think. I focused on Haman and his evil plot being recognized. I thought it would die with him."

"We must request the king to reverse the decree."

"I should return to the court."

Mordecai took hold of her hand. "Let us finish the task that has been set for today. In the morning, we go to the king."

The house was a little further than the palace, but still within Shushan. Esther paused as she saw the gallows where a body hung. "Have them remove that as soon as possible."

"In good time. It is a message to the enemies of

Israel." They turned their attention to the house. "I dare say this could be bigger than the palace."

"I am glad to put you in charge of it." Esther whistled. There was an arched opening through which they could see fruit trees. Further back, and taller, were four columns holding up a roof with copings adorned with red glazed tiles. The fruit trees were part of a garden between the entrance and the main doors into the house. She could hear water in a fountain but was more excited to explore inside.

"This wing will be perfect for me," Esther declared as they walked through an upper hallway. "There are seven bedrooms for my maidens, and this shall be mine." She walked into the large room with a balcony facing the mountains.

"We will make it perfect for you."

"See that there is a bathing house in the depths. I have grown to enjoy the pools beneath the palace." She turned and grinned at Mordecai. "We need our own cook. Esme frequently engages the help of Solique. Bring her into the house as well."

Mordecai lifted his brows. "Are you familiar with her?"

"I hear she has drawn your attention."

"She has better choices than someone like me." Mordecai chuckled.

Esther shook her head. "You are high minister to King Xerxes. There is no better choice for her."

Mordecai shook his head and Esther said no more. They continued. "Here is a good view." Mordecai stepped onto a balcony with an eastern view.

"You could watch the sunrise and moonrise."

"Me?"

"It is a good option for you. This is the largest room of this wing. Hatach can be close. You need other servants to assist you."

"What of my house in Susa?"

"We find someone worthy of it. As his most prized advisor, the king will want you close to the palace."

Mordecai made no comment. The tour continued. They met several servants and stopped a young man from taking things which did not belong to him. Esther finally covered a yawn.

"Return home. As the king stated, we will prepare your new house for your return from the summer capital. I will join you in the morning to go to him."

Chapter: Saving a Nation

With Mordecai beside her and the king's recent favor, Esther did not feel the qualms of her previous visit. Yet, her heart leapt when the king held the golden scepter toward her. Tears fell as she dropped to the floor before the throne. "My lord and my king, we must put away the mischief of Haman. We must break what he has devised against the Jews."

"Esther," the king took her hand, lifting her from the floor to set her on the chair beside him. "You need not cause yourself to suffer."

Esther kept hold of his hand. "If it please the king, and if I have found favor in your sight, let it be written to reverse the letters devised by Haman, the son of Hammedatha the Agagite, which he wrote to destroy the Jews in all the king's provinces. How can I endure to see evil come to my people?" She gazed at Mordecai. "To see the destruction of my kindred? My family?"

Xerxes' face darkened. "What is written in the king's name and sealed with the king's ring cannot be reversed." He looked to Mordecai. "What would a wise man say?"

Mordecai rubbed his beard a moment. "Let us write permission for the Jews to stand for their lives, to fight if need be.”

Xerxes nodded. “I have given Esther the house of Haman, and him they hanged upon the gallows because he dared lay his hand upon the Jews. Include that if it pleases you. Write in the king’s name and seal it with the signet. Let it stand against the words of Haman.”

Mordecai looked to Esther. At her nod, he reverenced the king with a bow and went to the scribes.

“He is the better man.” Xerxes muttered as they watched him hurry through the doorway.

Esther squeezed his hand. “Haman showed you what you wanted to see.”

“I should have known his intent. Be that as it may, my heart tells me I can trust Mordecai.”

“I have not known him to be dishonest or unfair.”

“He will join us in Persepolis, at least for a few weeks.”

“When do we leave?”

“The days of Karmabatas are upon us. We will leave at the Ahura Mazda.”

***

“We leave at the first of Tammuz,” Esther reverted to the Jewish name of the months as she ordered preparations.

Parisa laughed. “Good thing we started a few weeks ago. We could hardly have packed a case of clothes for you in two days.”

“I will be glad for cooler winds and the chance to visit the ocean.”

“What is that noise?” Esme called as she ran into the room. “What has happened?”

Esther went to the balcony, Parisa and Esme following. Though she couldn’t see into Susa, there were cries and a jumble of other noises. Not of sorrow, as the decree of Haman had produced. These sounds brought thoughts of joy to mind.

***

Mordecai hurried to the temple of the scribes, unwilling to wait for someone to attend him in a room in the palace. He ignored the images of their gods, but called for papyrus, lots of it. He held the ring of the king aloft. "Here is what you will write. On this twenty-third day of Sivan, of the Persian month Sakurrizis, the king's decree goes to all Jews, to the lieutenants, to the deputies and rulers of all provinces from India unto Ethiopia. Hear the king's command. All Jews are to gather themselves together, to stand for their life, to destroy, to slay, and to cause to perish all the power of the people and province that would assault them, both little ones and women, and to take the spoil of them for a prey. On the thirteenth day of the month of Adar, of the Persian month Miyakannas, all Jews are to be ready against that day to avenge themselves on their enemies."

The face of the scribe brightened. "By my honor, sir. You speak truth? There is to be no slaying of our friends and neighbors?"

Mordecai couldn't stop himself from smiling. "Write, that all may know the joy. There are one-hundred-twenty-seven provinces which need to hear our news. I will start on the languages but call for the others who wrote the message for Haman the Agagite."

He and the scribes wrote. They brought him parchments for the seal of the king. As the pile of completed letters grew, Mordecai called for Harbona and Carcas. "Prepare these letters for transport to each of the provinces. Be sure they are wrapped. Collect the most reliable of riders. Make use of the dromedary and Bactrian for the desert-most provinces. Send posts on horseback and mules to the other regions. Each lieutenant, deputy, governor, and ruler of all provinces are to receive these new edicts."

Carcas stared at the pile. "By what power is this to be done?"

Mordecai held his hand so the signet ring of the king could be seen. "By the highest powers of Persia, that of King Xerxes the Great and his High Minister Mordecai."

Carcas and Harbona bowed. "As it pleases my lord."

Mordecai laughed. "Save your obeisance for the king, just let it be known the Jews are to stand and fight against their enemies, if any dare to be enemies of the chosen people."

Mordecai himself took the letter into Susa, into the marketplace. "My friends, gather round." It was the sound of his voice they recognized, for the royal apparel of blue and white over a garment of fine purple linen was utterly foreign to them. He wore a great crown of gold on his head. "By now you have seen the body of Haman, the son of Hammedatha the Agagite, hanging on the gallows since yesterday. To me it has been given the role of High Minister, Vizier to King Xerxes the Great. Your Queen Esther brought our plight to the king, at risk for her life. Yes, she is your queen, the cousin I raised as my own daughter when her parents were killed. She has delivered you." Mordecai lifted the letter and read.

Tears of joy flowed down his face as he read the words, permitting them to stand together and fight if need be. Allowing others to stand with them. Light, gladness, joy, and honor filled the streets of Susa, the noise of them rising into the royal house of Shushan.

Chapter: A Royal Birth

Months passed. News flowed from every province into every city that the Jews and all who wanted to join in with their jubilations, feasted and celebrated. Even in Persepolis, news of the joy and gladness of the Jews brought delight in the day. Esther enjoyed the few days King Xerxes took her to the coast. As she began to show, his visits grew fewer, but Esther appreciated walking among the columns of the great palace with her maidens or taking the paths into the hills. Summer ended, bring cold down from the mountains. It was time to return to Shushan where a new home awaited her.

"It's perfect, Father Mordecai." Esther rubbed her stomach as she gazed at the transformation. The estate no longer resembled what had been given to her at Haman's death. Each room seemed inspired by a different exotic bird.

"Solique devised the plan." Mordecai led her into a sitting room. A sleek feline jumped onto a table.

"Cleo!" Esther exclaimed as she rubbed the cat's head. The deep blue walls of the peacock-inspired room were covered in part with gold shelves and stencils. The lounge and sofas would let a number of people sit comfortably.

Mordecai shook his head at the cat. "Hatach said an old man insisted on taking down the house he built for her in the garden at the palace and reassemble it here."

Esther picked up Cleo. "Must be the same man, Eldij, who built it for us."

"He is an old gardener. I've located him in a cottage with a few young slaves to teach them how to tend."

"It is good to be useful."

They moved to a yellow music room with images of an exotic macaw. White sofas formed a cozy listening center. The breeze coming through the open windows made her sigh. "I will spend many warm afternoons here."

"Your sleeping wing is this way. Solique spoke with your young women to see what would be best for all of you."

Her bed was built against the windows with a tall frame allowing gauze curtains to hang throughout the night as protection from insects. Pearls and gold inlays stood out against the deep cherry color of wood framing her bed. One wall had been painted the color of doves caught up in morning light while tapestries she'd seen in Queen Mother Atossa's rooms covered the rest of the walls. "How is this possible?" She touched the thick fabric.

"Hatach had it stored."

Esther stopped in front of a long cord with knots throughout. "I thought this had disappeared years ago."

"Your child will learn heritage of both his father and mother. He will be king, who knows what that will bring for our people."

Esther followed Mordecai to the balcony

overlooking the gardens and the marketplace. "How are our people?"

"They prepare. There has been word of contention. Men have been in the markets and other areas of Susa to raise war against the Jews."

Esther frowned. "Does anyone listen to them?"

"Not many, but I fear there will be some. It is best to be prepared."

"We have four months to be certain none of our people are without protection."

***

Winter arrived. As the days shortened, Esther's time was fulfilled. In the dark of night, her cries mingled with those of the women assisting in the birth. Dawn had just touched the eastern sky when a baby's wail broke through. Laughter and tears ensued as the boy was cleaned and laid upon his mother's chest. Jasmine placed pillows behind Esther so she could sit up. It took little urging for the baby to suckle. Esther sighed as she swept her fingers across his soft curling hair.

Mordecai stood without the chambers, and his face brightened when he heard the baby.

Solique opened the door. "A male child has been birthed."

"Hadassah?" He reverted to her Jewish name.

Solique nodded. "She is well. They will both sleep for some time."

Mordecai took her hand long enough to squeeze it. "Thank you." He strode from the house, continuing the road to the main gate. He went directly to the king's rooms, but the guards were gone, and the doors open. Xerxes wasn't there. He found Hatach in the small council room. "Where is the king?"

"News reached him of Queen Esther's child-bearing. He is at Apadana."

"She has given birth to a son."

Hatach stood. "This is good news."

***

Xerxes paced among the columns, running his hand through his hair. "There are many children in the harem, why does this one matter to me?"

Mordecai heard the question as he approached. "He is intended for your throne, heir of Persia."

Xerxes swerved. "He? It is a son?"

"Yes, my lord, you have a son. A strong child and healthy mother."

"May the gods be praised."

"Is Captain Horobath nearby?" Mordecai noticed morning light creeping across the floor.

"For what purpose?"

"You intend to take the throne from Darius. He, his caretaker, and his people must be sent away. Send them to the palace in Persepolis for now, but we should make plans to move them further still."

Xerxes nodded after a moment. "We need no confusion on whose line the throne will pass. Make the arrangements."

"Do you wish to see your new son?"

"I am satisfied for now. Bring him in seven days to the Halls of the People. He shall be named."

"Our people have a practice if you will incline to hear. On the eighth day, I would like to have him circumcised. There is an old priest in Susa. He will perform the ritual to honor YHWH."

"As you wish. The boy will be raised steeped in wisdom of both his families."

***

Mordecai returned to Esther. "I am pleased to see you, daughter." Mordecai wrapped his hands around Esther's hand.

She smiled, then yawned. "Oh my. Have you seen him?"

"He is perfect. Your nurse says he has lusty appetite and healthy cries."

"His hair is curly. He will look like the king."

"The city has been rejoicing in the birth announcement. They are eager to see him in a week."

"The king names him."

"He is pleased and sends his regards. I told him of our plan for circumcision."

"He agrees?"

"He has not opposed. Rest well. I will see you in a few days."

"Are you away? Winter is not a good time for travel."

"Our day draws ever closer. I have not heard from all provinces. Do they need weapons? More soldiers? There are few I trust with such knowledge. I must be one to go. I will return before the day of your son's announcement."

He left her without concern. Her color had already returned to her cheeks and it had not been a day. He headed to the stables. Three others waited for him. "Horses are our best option for this time of year." He told the stablemaster to prepare what they would need. "Include a horse blanket for each."

With the arrangements being worked, he went to the three advisors. "Master Carcas, Master Altier, and Master Nader." He greeted them all. "Have you mapped your journey?"

"May the weather hold until our return," Altier wrapped a turban around his pointed hat. The others nodded.

"Good. Return with news as soon as you can. We send supplies and soldiers at your bidding."

Carcas secured a flask on his luggage. "My young aid, Costeson, says sons of Haman the Agagite have been quarrelling in ale houses in the southern portion of Susa."

"Look into it when you return. Their father spoiled their hearts."

***

Days passed faster than Esther could track. Her body was weary, but how could she sleep when the tiny body of her son wiggled against her. "He smiles, did you see?" She waved for Jasmine.

Jasmine let him grip her finger. "He is strong."

Khepri arrived to take Esther to the bath house, but she ended up sitting beside her, holding the boy. He didn't seem to mind all their attention.

"My dear queen, you need rest, as does your son. I will take him." The nurse disturbed their play.

"Not yet," Esther put her hand on his belly. His legs kicked, making her laugh. "I remember how you love to kick."

The nurse took him from her. "A schedule grows a healthy disposition. I will bring him before you sleep tonight."

"Tomorrow will be his naming day. There will be celebration across the city."

***

Preparations started early. After an hour with Khepri, Esther's skin glowed. Banu outlined her eyes with kohl, drawing curled wings up to her hairline to mimic the sweep of curls across her head. Zarak, golden dust, sparkled like glitter on her smooth skin.

"A perfect complement," Parisa exclaimed as she brought a golden tunic to be worn over a blue draped skirt and top with gold stripes. Leather stars decorated the stripes.

Esther's attention drifted from her dress when the nurse brought her son. The woman wore gray while the child had been wrapped in blue matching his mother. Esther wanted to hold him, but the ritual put her in the lead of a procession while the nurse and baby came after her maidens.

Hall of the People was the eastern side of Apadana. Rather than the private trail she'd taken to go to the king uncalled, this procession went forth through the gardens, into the eastern court, then through to the Apadana. They walked the steps to the upper level and met King Xerxes in the waiting area to the balcony overlooking Susa. King Xerxes wore a long kandys coat a darker shade of blue over his white vest with a red sash. Unlike Esther's simple pattern of stripes, his coat was pleated with concentric circles and lotus blossoms painted into the fabric.

"Queen Esther," Xerxes' voice boomed. He put his hands on her arms and greeted her with traditional kisses to both cheeks. "You are radiant."

"It is an honor to be here with you," she grinned, remembering how well he enjoyed his formal ceremonies.

"Bring the child," he ordered, keeping one hand on Esther's arm.

The nurse walked forward. The baby fussed as he

was lifted closer to his father, but then Xerxes' hair and beard had the little one reaching out with pudgy hands.

Esther took hold of his waving fists and kissed them.

Xerxes laughed, releasing Esther to hold his son. "A fine boy you are." He smiled at Esther. "Come, let us introduce him to the people."

From the elevation of the balcony, Esther could see many had arrived to celebrate the new birth. King Xerxes kept a firm grip on the boy but lifted him high. "The gods have attended to our needs and our wants. A fine boy, your future king. I name you Artexerxes. May the outpourings of bounty and blessing descend upon you. May wisdom, strength, and honor grow in you. May the nations of the world bow to you, as they have your father and father's father." He lowered Artexerxes so he could see his face. The king leaned down and kissed the warm forehead. Artexerxes took advantage and closed his fists around the beard that tickled his face. Xerxes laughed as Esther reached over to disentangle them. "Thank you."

The warmth of his eyes was more than freeing him from the tug of his son. Esther nodded, holding her baby close. Far too soon, they retreated from the balcony to the cries and blessings of the people.

Xerxes stayed close. "I am pleased. What manner of gift would you appreciate?"

She traced her finger across the baby's cheek. "A horse that I may ride with our son one day."

"The stables have room for another steed." He nodded. "It shall be done."

With the formal proclamation over, the procession moved to the grounds. Pavilions and tents were set throughout the gardens. The men moved into areas closer to the king's palace. Esther joined Khepri, Jasmine, and Banu in her pavilion. "Where is Esme and Douika? Parisa is getting a lighter stole for me." Esther waved her hand for a breeze. "Warmer today than we thought it would be."

"Esme will bring food for us." Jasmine held Artexerxes as Esther settled on a couch. "There are many cooks for the festival. She wants to be sure we receive only the best."

"Good thing her grasp of Persian has improved over the years." It had been a battle and they laughed.

They were finished eating when Esther noticed men hovering nearby. They never approached closer but gave glances toward her pavilion and huddled in private conversation. From their similar coloring, they could be brothers or cousins. Why were they in the ladies' area of the festivities? Esther waved for Hatach. He leaned over to hear her. "The group of men with black stripes across their robes, who are they?"

Hatach' jaw tightened. "They are sons of Haman and his wife, Zeresh. I am not sure what they are doing here."

"Go to them. Be sure they are in peace."

But, as soon as the men noticed attention had turned to them, they disbanded into the crowds. Though the festival waxed with merriment, Esther lost her pleasure in it. "I want to take Artexerxes home. We have another big day tomorrow. Sleep is in order."

***

The quiet morning held a touch of cold. This procession differed from the first. Queen Esther wore a simple robe of blue. Nurse held Artexerxes wrapped in a silken green blanket. The king had other business

221

preventing him from joining them.

The old priest, Ebenezer, welcomed them into his home. It was a small room with benches on three walls. They could see through a breezeway to a kitchen in the back.

"Please, place him on the table."

Nurse glanced at Esther, her eyes wide. A sharp knife and a towel were laid on the table along with a pitcher of water. Esther smiled and nodded.

The nurse did so, then backed away. "I wait outside." She hurried away.

Mordecai squeezed Esther's shoulder.

The priest undressed the baby. 'As Father Abraham, and Father Isaac, and Father Jacob so it is our duty to follow and obey YHWH. His hand of blessing can already be seen upon all of us." The deed was done swiftly. Artexerxes screamed and his little body quivered. Khepri brought a vial of oils to tend the wound. Within minutes, he had calmed to a whimper. Esther wrapped him in the blanket and held him close, cooing in a singsong tone as she rocked him gently.

The priest took hold of Artexerxes arm. "Babies heal quickly, and they carry no memory."

Mordecai bowed. "Your service is appreciated."

"I will soon sleep with my fathers." He sat with a grunt. "There are few priests of the tribe of Levi remaining in Persia. It is to our home we must look."

"Pray that the time may be soon." Mordecai glanced at Esther. "Take him outside to the nurse. She will be eager to see his is safe."

Esther chuckled. "That she is."

As they were leaving, Esther heard mention the date of the attack. Perhaps they should invite the old man to the palace. She looked around the neighborhood. Or his neighbors would protect him. She saw several standing in front of their homes, or inside the doorway.

Nurse scurried to her side. "You chose not to go through with it," she exclaimed.

Esther shook her head. "He circumcised quickly. See, he is safe." She allowed the nurse to take him.

"I am glad that is over."

They returned to Esther's house in Shushan. It was later in the day when Mordecai caught up with her. He entered with a bow.

Esther laughed. "There is no need for that, Father. I am glad to see you. How did your errand go?"

"We are prepared. The day of destruction will not be as Haman and his kind hoped."

"It will be for rejoicing. May it come swiftly."

224

Chapter: The Days of Purim

The thirteenth day of Miyakannas, the month of Adar by the Jewish calendar, dawned with thick clouds in a starless sky. Pale light marked the end of night. Nader stumbled into the courtyard. "Mordecai," he called

Mordecai wasn't asleep, nor were the two columns of soldiers awaiting direction.

"Nader, what happened?" Mordecai ran to his friend, then turned to the closest soldier. "Fetch a doctor. Swiftly." Mordecai helped Nader sit on the grass. "What happened?"

"There is no time," Nader gasped, holding his side. "My wound is not mortal. Haman's sons mean to retake his house. Send your soldiers to protect the queen."

"They would be fools to think they could attack the queen and prince and survive."

"They are maddened. They listen to no council."

"Captain," Mordecai called for the man with the crimson feather in his head gear. A thick leather vest protected the man's bare chest. For weapons, he carried a long bow with a quiver of arrows and a slender spear.

"Minister," the man bowed.

"Take your troupe to the queen's palace. We hear there will be an attempt to overthrow our control in order to return it to Haman's wife and sons."

"They will die trying." The captain dipped his head.

Mordecai remained with Nader as the soldiers left. Nader pushed him. "You should not stay here."

Mordecai laughed. "I will leave when I am ready. Tell me what happened."

"I've heard them in the ale houses, Parshandatha and his brothers, talking to any who will listen. I saw him on the street after dark. He wears a weapon on his side. I followed him into a different ale house. He spoke briefly, drawing a small crowd. Among their babel I heard him say he means to take back what belongs to them and their mother, Zeresh."

"How many of them?"

"There are ten sons."

***

"Mistress, we are being moved to a safer location."

Esther woke as Jasmine shook her shoulder. "What happened?"

"I do not know. A troupe of soldiers have come to the house and we are moving further inside."

Esther stood and Jasmine helped her into a gray robe. "Where is my son?" Esther asked as she tied a sash at her waist.

Jasmine led Esther from her bedroom. "He is in the sitting room on the second floor."

Esther nodded. "It is an interior room. Have more imperial guards been brought into the house?" A thought made her stumble. "The entrance to the bathhouse. You must find Hatach, be sure to remind him to set soldiers in that long corridor."

Jasmine's eyes widened. "Who would know about the subterranean entrance?"

"Those who lived here before us. I will make my way to the sitting room. Hurry, tell Hatach."

Esther hurried through dimly lit hallways and stairwells until she reached the second floor. The nurse held Artexerxes, who left them no doubt he did not like being pulled from sleep.

"Why have they sent soldiers? This is a home, not a military compound." The nurse questioned as she held the baby tight.

Esther took him. "I don't know. Father Mordecai would only do so if it were necessary." She walked and rocked her son who continued to fuss. She started to sing, and his arms slowed. The red in his face faded as he calmed.

The nurse smiled. "He knows his mother's voice."

Esme hurried into the room followed by a servant with a laden tray. "I brought breakfast, cold lamb and sweet bread. They would not allow me to bake a proper meal. I could not even grab a pitcher of juice."

"Did they say what is going on?" The nurse peaked her head out of the room.

Esme moved closer to Esther. "They tried to break in. Someone's been killed, them, not us."

Esther held Artexerxes close to her chest. "They are ones who want to fight against the Jews."

***

With Nader in the care of a physician, Mordecai put on the royal uniform and walked from Shushan down into Susa. The markets were empty, but fighting could be heard further south.

"You should not be walking alone, Minister

Mordecai.”

A woman’s voice snapped at him. He turned to Zeresh who was hiding in a doorway. He shook his head. “It would have been better for you to take your sons to a new city. They have talents. You all could start fresh.”

“Why start fresh when we can reclaim what is ours?”

“The king declared otherwise.”

“He is a fool. Look who his queen is.”

“She is the right one for such a time as this.”

“That may be. Perhaps, killing you will give me satisfaction enough.” She drew a dagger from her belt. Before she could step closer, an arrow whizzed through the air and punctured her chest.

A black man in soldier uniform moved from a market stall into the open. “Did you think the chief minister would be unprotected?”

Zeresh gasped. Her metal blade clattered on the ground when she dropped it. She staggered against the building and slowly slid to rest on the ground. Mordecai clenched his lips as he watched breath go out, but she no longer breathed in. She was dead.

“Thank you.” He turned to the other man.

“Master Nader sent me to follow you. I was only to approach if there was need. Shall we return to the palace?”

***

Sammy sat up. “She died? What about her sons? Did they die too?”

Sharine placed her hand on the book in her lap and nodded at her grandson. “All ten of them. They thought to have mastery over the Jews, but the Jews gained mastery over those who hated them. All throughout

Persia, the officials and governors and royal agents helped the Jews."

Sammy's eyes widened. "What about the others?"

Sharine returned to the book.

***

It was hours later when Jasmine rejoined Esther. "The worst is over, for now." Jasmine sat with a sigh. "Soldiers say almost five hundred of those who rose against the Jews have been killed. Others have gone into hiding."

"So, they can attack another day?" Esther touched the soft cheek of Artexerxes. "We need peace. We need to know there is no reason to fear."

"The king asks you to join him for a meal. See what he thinks should happen."

Khepri and Parisa arrived in the doorway. Khepri rubbed her arms. "The bathhouse has been cleansed of this morning's evil doings. We should prepare you for dinner at the king's palace."

Esther went with them, but the thought of someone dying in the corridors of the subterranean rooms made her shiver. Banu wrapped a turban on Esther's head to keep her hair dry. Warm water bathed in minerals soothed Esther's spirit as she washed. She dressed in a simple long gown of pale blue with a matching cloak. Once her hair was plaited, Banu pinned a hair cover with a gold weave band around her head.

The sun hovered in the west when Esther left her place and walked toward Shushan. Mordecai joined her. At the Gate of Darius, they turned.

Mordecai breathed. "It will be a quiet night. Tomorrow will be a day of rejoicing."

"Are there still those who would harm the Jews?"

229

"Some, yes."

"Then perhaps tomorrow should be another day of battle. Finish this once and for all."

Mordecai kissed her temple. "Not for all time, but our time. We will petition the king."

Xerxes met her as they passed into the palace. He grasped her hands. "My queen, you are well? I did not want to hear of wicked men attacking your home."

Esther accepted his greeting of a kiss to both cheeks. "The soldiers protected us well. We heard no disturbance."

"I am pleased." He took the lead, followed by Mordecai and then Esther as they walked to the palace garden. A pavilion had been erected. Torches nearby provided enough heat to take the chill from the air. The king sat on a short stool with a thick cushion, then reached for Esther, for her to take the cushion to his right. Mordecai sat across from them.

"Have you heard reports from the captain?" Mordecai enquired after their goblets of wine were filled.

"Indeed." The king raised his cup. "In Susa, the Jews have killed and destroyed five hundred men and also the ten sons of Haman. What have they done in the rest of the king's provinces? Now, what is your wish, Queen Esther? It shall be granted you. Your request will be fulfilled."

"Reports suggest there may be more who hate the Jews, who wait to cause trouble when we have turned to rejoicing. We should send a message. Let the sons of Haman hang on gallows for all to see. Declare the cost of rising against us. If it please the king, let the Jews of Susa be allowed tomorrow to do according to this day's edict. Then, on the fifteenth, we will celebrate with great joy and gladness all that has been saved."

Xerxes nodded, and turned to a servant. "Send Hatach to me, along with a scribe."

As they ate their meal of lamb roasted in rosemary and ginger, the scribe recorded the words of the king and Mordecai, preparing an edict to go through Susa that night.

Hatach bowed. "I will see it done."

***

"Another day of battle?" Sammy leaned forward eagerly.

Sharine shook her head. "A small one, and in Susa only. Another three hundred were killed as they tried to harm the Jews living in the region."

Rachel frowned. "Why would they do that if they saw how bad things went the day before?"

Sharine laughed. "Good question, dear. Just as hate is difficult to understand, so are the actions of those who allow hate to consume them. Mordecai recorded everything that happened and sent letters throughout the provinces. Reports came to the king that seventy-five thousand throughout Persia fought against the Jews and were killed. Most places celebrated the next day, the fourteenth of Adar, while Susa waited to celebrate until the fifteenth."

Sammy gasped. "That's why we have two days of celebrations."

"It is. We commemorate the fasting and pray for victory over our enemies."

Sammy giggled. "I like when we get to heckle Haman in services."

"What about Esther? Did she and the king have a happy ending? Were they in love?" Rachel flopped back on the couch with a sigh.

"The Megillah does not give us the end of their story, only the story of Purim. The king liked Esther well enough to make her his queen, but he had many wives and many other concubines. History tells us King Xerxes was assassinated by Artabanus, his royal bodyguard commander. Though we do not know for certain about Queen Esther, it is said she was murdered as well. Their son, Artexerxes, would eventually become king. It is he who provided Nehemiah what was needed to rebuild the walls of Jerusalem. Perhaps it is the influence of his mother and Mordecai that led him to look favorably on Nehemiah and the Jewish nation with their desire to return to the land of their fathers." Sharine closed the book. Family sat around her. Camille curled in one corner of the couch, allowing the dog, Sedgwick, to lounge beside her, his head in her lap.

Isaiah stood from his seat on the steps leading down into the room. He placed the kippah on his head and bowed in prayer. "Compassionate one, all our lacks and needs are revealed and known before You. Behold, the time is right for You to redeem us, to grace us, to have compassion on us, in the fulness of Your mercy and infiniteness of Your love."

Judy Lewis' authentic Hamantaschen recipe for Purim:

4 c. Flour, 3 t baking powder, 3/4 c. sugar .... blend. 4 eggs beaten, 1/2 c. oil, 1/4 c. pineapple juice. Mix all ingredients gently and then chill 30-45 minutes. Roll out until about 1/4 inch thick. Cut into 3-to-4-inch rounds. Fill each round with about 1.5 tsp filling. Pie filling cut into smaller pieces is great. Fold into a triangle around the filling. Cook at 350 for 20 minutes total (turn part way through). Cool before eating as filling is HOT! and eat or freeze. Apx 24 cookies. All fillings are great - traditional are blueberry, cherry or raspberry. Even more traditional are prune and poppy. But get creative.

234

Thank you for joining me in Esther's story. This has been a labor of love. Research into the ancient Persian Empire has been fascinating.

To sign up for my Newsletter, visit www.LaurieLeeFairyLand.com

Intrigued with Esther's story? *By the Fruit of Her Hands* series presents the lives of three Old Testament Matriarchs. Rahab has no qualms with enjoying the company of visitors who stay at her inn. But as talk of desert ghosts increases fear within Jericho. Someone she doesn't understand is drawing her. When she finds spies from Israel within the walls of Jericho, she makes a rash choice to hide them. Can her choice save her from the destruction that has been ordained? *Jewel of Jericho: Rahab's Story* is the first book in this series. Click here for more.

About the Author: Laurie Boulden was born in Philadelphia, grew up in Oklahoma, and now resides in Florida. She is an educator and a writer. Writing has been her passion since childhood, so the opportunity to publish is thrilling. Her family consists of her dog, Sandy, and two cats. Will there be a third cat? Or a puppy in the future some time? Maybe so. She believes a good story is food for the soul. Her favorite quote is "Not all those who wander are lost". She loves to wander.

Connect with the Author:

- On Facebook
- On Instagram
- On Twitter

- Website

Books by Laurie Boulden

- Hidden Gems (suspense)
- By the Fruit of Her Hands: Jewel of Jericho
- By the Fruit of Her Hands: Mistress of Moab
- By the Fruit of Her Hands: Journeying the Walls of Jericho
- Cookies, Cocoa, and Capers (Christmas rom com)
- A Time to Die (time travel suspense)
- Cowboy Blessing (sweet romance)
- The Maxwell Murders (suspense)

Also check out books by Laurie Lee

- Cinderella Spell (fantasy)